Guardian's Vengeance

Anna Gabriel Book 1

Georgia Wagner

Text Copyright © 2024 Georgia Wagner

Publisher: Greenfield Press Ltd

The right of Georgia Wagner to be identified as author of the Work has been asserted in accordance with the Copyright, Designs and Patents Act 1988

All rights reserved.

The book is copyright material and must not be copied, reproduced, transferred, distributed, leased, licensed or publicly performed or used in any way except as specifically permitted in writing by the publishers, as allowed under the terms and conditions under which it was purchased or as strictly permitted by applicable copyright law. Any unauthorised distribution or use of this text may be a direct infringement of the author's and publisher's rights and those responsible may be liable in law accordingly.

'Guardian's Vengeance' is a work of fiction. Names, characters, businesses, organisations, places, events, and incidents either are the product of the author's imagination or are used fictitiously. Any resemblance to actual persons, living or dead, and events or locations is entirely coincidental.

Contents

1. Chapter 1 — 1
2. Chapter 2 — 13
3. Chapter 3 — 29
4. Chapter 4 — 47
5. Chapter 5 — 61
6. Chapter 6 — 74
7. Chapter 7 — 87
8. Chapter 8 — 100
9. Chapter 9 — 115
10. Chapter 10 — 130
11. Chapter 11 — 141
12. Chapter 12 — 154
13. Chapter 13 — 162

14.	Chapter 14	182
15.	Chapter 15	192
16.	Chapter 16	200
17.	Chapter 17	218
18.	Chapter 18	234
19.	Chapter 19	252
20.	Chapter 20	256
21.	Chapter 21	266
22.	Chapter 22	281
23.	Chapter 23	297
24.	Chapter 24	323
25.	What's Next for Anna?	331
26.	Also by Georgia Wagner	333
27.	Also by Georgia Wagner	335
28.	Also by Georgia Wagner	337
29.	Want to know more?	339
30.	About the Author	341

Chapter 1

Anna Gabriel watched as the man with the guitar case got off the bus, hefting his bag.

She knew she shouldn't involve herself. Her hand gripped her phone, and the burner's screen displayed the single-word text message that had prompted her to travel across the country on a two-day bus ride from Cleveland to Yosemite.

She lowered the phone. Staring at it wouldn't make the cryptic text message any clearer. She returned her attention to the man with the guitar case who was now standing on the sidewalk.

She sighed, rubbing at the bridge of her nose and yawning as her head rested against the cool glass of the overnight bus. It wasn't her job to get involved--not anymore. Five years ago, she'd been discharged, and while the civilian life hadn't suited her, she'd managed to get by without sticking her nose in other peoples' business.

She brushed her dark hair behind her ears. Though she was only thirty, the fringe on the left side had a long strand of pure-white amidst the black. A single streak of white, like a slip of silver in ebony. She was passably attractive with sharp cheekbones, a celestial nose, and piercing green eyes, but she never used her looks as an advantage. To some, she might have looked like a church girl, but the bone-frog and trident tattoo on her forearm often quickly deteriorated such assumptions.

Her femininity had been the cause of multiple headaches while in the male-dominated SEALs. But it had served well on more than one mission.

It was always about the mission. But now?

She'd spotted the M4-Carbine barrel before he'd zipped up the guitar case. She'd heard the distinct sound of rattling ammunition from the man's backpack. The other passengers hadn't noticed, but they weren't accustomed to the chime of clinking bullets like the notes of a familiar piece of music she could hum along too. Memories of her time in Sanaa, Yemen came drifting back. Images flashed through her mind of the shooting in the bazaar. Thirty-five dead. Fifteen wounded.

She'd ignored her instincts then, too.

That time, because of orders. But now?

She sighed, her breath fogging the glass, her eyes still fixated on the man with the guitar case. A gray man. A term often used for an unsub with no particular discernible features. He was conspicuous in how inconspicuous he was.

She watched as he paused on the curb by the bus stop, adjusting the strap of his guitar case. He had brown hair brushed to the side, was of an average build, and his features were unremarkable.

She also scanned for a trailing entity.

Men like this, men with a plan, didn't often work alone.

She scanned figures in the bus, watching, waiting.

The bus began to roll again. And yet still she waited—it's what she would've done. To make sure no one was following.

Then she spotted him.

A second man with a backpack, also with dark hair and unremarkable features.

He pulled the emergency stop and hastened to the front of the vehicle. "Getting off," he muttered to the bus driver.

The driver issued a series of expletives but allowed the man to disembark.

Two of them now.

As the man began to walk away, Anna made a split-second decision. She grabbed her backpack and followed.

The doors had closed again, and as she approached the front, the driver gave her a stink-eye. "You too?"

"Yeh," she said in her usual, curt mode of speaking. Anna slipped a tenner to the driver, which seemed to cheer him up a bit. Money had never much mattered to her. She had little use for it and less respect. "Give me thirty seconds before I get off?" she said.

The driver frowned at the tenner. She added another.

He nodded, hitting his hazards and allowing the bus to linger by the stop.

It was early enough on the overnight bus that most of the passengers didn't notice this temporary respite.

Anna, on the other hand, rubbed the sleep from her eyes. She noticed the driver staring at one of her tattoos. He looked up at her. "Frogman?" he asked.

She shook her head. "Not anymore."

He nodded, impressed. "I was a recruiting assistant for a couple years. Didn't know there were any female SEALS."

"There aren't," she said simply. She tried to keep her tone polite but clear. She wasn't interested in conversation. She tugged at the sleeve of her blue wind-breaker, attempting to disguise the ink.

The man with the backpack was a good distance ahead, and Anna couldn't see the man with the guitar case anymore.

"So... did they let you in as a sort of policy hire, or something?" The driver asked.

She wasn't sure if he was trying to insult her, and she didn't really care. Facing gunfire on three continents put things in perspective. But his comment did irk her somewhat. She'd gone through BUDS, SEAL training school, just like everyone else. She'd wanted to quit, just like everyone else. And she hadn't, just like everyone who made it to the end of hell week. She still had the scars from some of the more intense tests during training. She'd broken three ribs on the second day, but hadn't told anyone. She hadn't wanted to be discharged. It had been months before anyone had found out. She had many trophies like this—hard won tokens of suffering she kept closer than any medal or ribbon, as close as skin.

Not to mention the other souvenirs from three tours.

"Demolitions?" he said, still not getting the hint.

"Sniper," she replied, with a sigh, hoping he'd drop it.

"You went to sniper school?"

"Mhmm," she said, still peering through the bus window, and watching the two men.

"No way!"

She shrugged, and could now feel the bus driver watching her a bit more closely. She hadn't just gone to sniper school. She'd done demolitions as well and had eventually worked in more than one inter-agency task force. She'd started with the SEALs but had eventually been exclusively assigned to a specialized operations unit. Or, as it was conventionally known, Black Ops—a government assassin for hire.

But all of that was behind her.

She considered returning to her seat on the bus, going back to sleep. This wasn't her problem anymore—wasn't that what the US government had decided when they'd dishonorably discharged her?

But again, flashes of that bazaar jolted through her mind, and her stomach twisted.

"You here for the concert?" he asked.

She shot him a glance. "What concert?"

He waved his hand dismissively. "Some big country star is stopping by this podunk place. They've set up some tents."

"Huh. Yeah, I might check it out."

The bus driver hit the button for the doors and allowed them to slowly slide open. The cool, early morning breeze gusted into the bus.

"Thanks," she said. And then she stepped through the doors, following the two men into the dark of the early morning.

She regulated her heart rate with each step, focusing on her breathing, and keeping her mind on one task at a time. She kept a safe distance, but she didn't want to lose sight of the two men.

Yup. Definitely a pair.

They were now walking side by side at the end of the block.

It wasn't strictly her business... but men who had guns and bullets on a bus? Especially where one trails the other to keep an eye out for pursuers?

She knew trouble when she saw it.

And that was the curse of civilian life, wasn't it?

She spotted the trouble, but most could ignore it, or not notice to begin with. Ignorance was bliss, some said, but knowledge was obligation to her.

A flash of memory returned like they so often did. Sometimes, she thought she stayed on the move to try and outrun her own thoughts.

In this memory, she spotted the smiling, brown face of a Pakistani billionaire's son. The man's money had funded a terrorist operation that had seen six American tourists tortured and killed. She'd made first contact at a night club.

She'd lured him into the bathroom.

He'd never left.

She had.

One of many successful missions. If that's what one could call them. Mission. She wasn't sure anymore.

And so she kept moving, leaving the thought behind her, though eventually she knew it would return like a haunting poltergeist.

GUARDIAN'S VENGEANCE

Anna kept a steady pace, trying to stay within the shadows. She was thankful for the darkness of the early morning hour as it allowed her to remain undetected. She stayed far enough away that she couldn't make out any details of the two men's conversation, but close enough that she could still track them.

Anna followed, staying low and taking cover behind the occasional stone wall or sidewalk-planted tree. She stayed in the shadows, out of sight and not making a sound. She was careful not to step on any twigs or leaves or urban detritus that might alert them to her presence.

As they rounded the corner, Anna could now see a large white pavilion set up in the middle of a field. The sun was slowly rising, casting an orange-pink hue over the morning sky. A single car was parked out front.

The men stopped at the entrance to the tent and stood there for a moment before one of them opened the flimsy, plywood door, and stepped inside. Anna watched as he reached into his pocket and pulled out something small. Then, the two men slipped through the front entrance of the large, temporary tent disappearing from sight.

She cautiously approached the shelter herself, keeping an eye out for any signs of movement from within or around it.

Again, as she moved in the cold morning, part of her longed for the warmth of the overnight bus.

She often slept on buses or planes.

There was something strange in the way the motion soothed her. She didn't own a home, didn't rent a place, and spent most of her time in motels. She had a small, C-class RV as a mobile home base. The RV was currently parked in a campground in Yosemite. That was where she'd been headed before she'd spotted the man with the M4-Carbine.

She didn't have a weapon on her; though, she'd killed enough men without one to consider her bare hands sufficient tools of the trade.

Was she just being paranoid?

She paused in the shadow of the large, white tent, scowling. Her hand reflexively stroked at her left hip where she would normally have strapped her Glock 22. She was left-handed but could aim and fire well enough with both.

She stepped to the entrance of the tent, watching as both men stood in the shadows of the pale awning.

They were examining the tent, both of them scanning the area. The one with the guitar case pointed in one corner of the place and muttered something under his breath to the other.

This second wore a grim expression, hefted his backpack, and nodded.

She frowned, glancing around for signs of any employees of the park district, but none were visible. The two men were murmuring softly to each other. The one with the guitar case looked the more nervous of the two.

"...This afternoon," he was saying in a dull voice. "Three PM."

"You sure there'll be enough people here by then?"

"Mhmm. Drunk too. Should give us plenty of time."

The second man wagged his head. He then raised his hand like a finger gun and mouthed the word bang as he pointed in the direction of the wooden stage.

Anna still remained in the shadow of the threshold, keeping watch.

One thing she'd learned as a sniper was how to sit still for long periods of time. People didn't truly appreciate the art of doing absolutely nothing for long, extended intervals. The smallest motion, even scratching at one's nose, in the wrong setting, could draw all sorts of unwanted attention. It could cost someone their life.

She knew the art of blending into her surroundings, of becoming just a stationary piece of the, admittedly scenic, surroundings.

Even the road to Yosemite was lined with large mountains, and though the trees behind her, circling the tent, weren't as large as the famed, giant sequoias of Yosemite, they were larger than any she'd seen back in Ohio where she'd boarded the bus.

Just then, she heard a sound.

The two men inside the tent went still. And all of them tensed, staring at the back of the stage in anticipation.

Someone was coming.

Chapter 2

The gunmen seemed to relax a second later as two more men emerged from behind the stage. These newcomers were dressed similarly to the first duo. They also wore dark shirts and had stubble. They were also of average height and both looked as if they were of Middle Eastern descent. They spoke English without an accent, though, as they raised their hands and greeted the men she'd been following.

She remained motionless, like a stone gargoyle in the shadows.

"Took you long enough," one was saying.

The other chuckled, "Late, like always."

The four men shared embraces and kisses on either side of one another's cheeks. A familiar greeting from her second tour. Her mind continued to piece together the information. Turkish? Iranian? She frowned.

The two newcomers also had black backpacks and one of the men, she realized, had a gun jammed into his waistband. She could make out the faint indentation of the device.

The man who'd withdrawn the small item she'd spotted earlier, extended it towards the two newcomers. "It's all there. We start at Three."

"Three? Early, isn't it? This place won't be crowded yet."

The four men faced each other, speaking in quiet but confident voices as if they were used to this sort of thing. As if they'd done it before.

But done what? What were they here for?

Suddenly, there was a sound. A creaking of hinges. Anna glanced sharply towards the opposite side of the tent, where a second, plywood door, was set in the fabric of the white awning.

The four men tensed and looked over sharply as well.

A figure had emerged from behind the stage left curtain. She was yawning and scratching at her jaw. She had on a bright fleece with a logo on the shirt that Anna didn't recognize, but that made her guess this woman was somehow involved in coordinating the event.

The woman went still by the stage as she spotted the four men.

She hesitated. "I... I'm sorry, but this area is closed until the concert."

The men just stared at her.

And as Olivia watched their postures, she felt a shiver crawl up her spine. Something in the atmosphere had shifted. The men had hunched backs, and leaned forward with an almost predatory carriage, like vultures stooped over carrion.

They didn't speak.

"I... I'm sorry," the woman on the stage said hesitantly. "Did you hear me?"

The men remained quiet, watching her.

She frowned now. She was middle-aged, with pleasant, cherubic features. Her eyes were tired and her hair was uncombed, but she looked as if she likely smelled of soap and peppermint.

Anna was briefly reminded of her own mother. They hadn't spoken in... what was it, ten years?

The men slowly began to advance towards the woman. They moved in unison as if they were used to this sort of thing, or perhaps as if their predatory instincts were attuned to one another.

She watched as one of the men began to reach into his backpack, the zipper brushing against his pale fingers.

She wasn't sure what they intended, but she'd seen and heard enough to move.

Even if the woman hadn't reminded her of her mother, Anna wouldn't have stood by. Not now. She'd gotten off the bus and *that* meant consequences.

She stepped forward, casually and cleared her throat.

"Excuse me!" she called out.

The four men had nearly cornered the frightened, middle-aged concert worker.

But at the sound behind them, they whirled around to face her.

Each of them frowned as they spotted her.

Anna raised a hand and gave a little wave. She kept her hands visible to show she wasn't armed. Instead of retreating, though, she closed the distance. Not fast. No... speed could alarm. Sometimes, if one took a few steps over a long period, as opposed to a single step fast it was perceived as less threatening, though in reality, it was far more dangerous.

She closed the distance slowly, hands outstretched, smiling broadly.

"Soooo sorry!" she exclaimed, giving a bubbly little laugh and a giggle. She held a hand to her lips as if embarrassed. She brushed her strand of pale white hair behind one ear. "This isn't the restroom, is it?" She gave another laugh, vaguely gesturing to the men's tent.

More camouflage. Another component of her training. It was a little-known fact, but every single member of the special operations taskforce she'd been involved in had endured nearly a year of professional acting and improvisation lessons.

Physical camouflage was crucial. But social camouflage was just as important.

She faked a small stumble, exclaiming with a little laugh. "Oh, clumsy me," she said with a chuckle. "I think I'm early. Where is everyone?" She looked around and pretended to stumble again. Gave a little hiccup, and once more pressed her hand to her mouth.

The four men, who'd tensed at her arrival, began to relax.

A pretty, drunk Californian girl wasn't a threat.

She was just more prey.

"You really can't be in here!" the employee was saying, still flustered, but sticking to her job. "I'm sorry, but the concert isn't until two PM."

"We know," said one of the men, glancing back. "It's going to be fun."

"Very fun," another one of the men said, flashing a grin.

They were in their twenties, no older and no younger.

Young men, Middle-Eastern descent, culturally similar, given the greeting she'd witnessed, and armed. Two groups, each one with a trailing partner who'd kept an eye on the other. Hidden weapons.

The information flooded her mind rapidly. She examined it with cold detachment.

Internally, her mind processed; externally, she wore a dopey grin and spoke in her bubbly, Valley-girl voice. "Oh, it is going to be fun, isn't it?"

"Is anyone with you?" asked the man with the guitar case. He had dark eyes. Like lumps of coal, or stains of ink. He watched her, unblinking.

Again, she was reminded of a vulture.

"Hmm? Hey!" she yelled suddenly.

One of the men had been reaching for the employee's arm. He frowned at her exclamation. The employee tried to scamper back, but the man tripped her, sending the woman unceremoniously to the ground.

The other men laughed.

Anna ignored it, wanting to draw the attention back to herself.

"Are you guys working the concert or something?" She tottered a bit again, pretending as if she couldn't quite stand on her own two feet.

The men were all watching her closely now. One had a gun in his hand but kept it hidden under his shirt.

She was now only ten paces away. Close enough. It was already too late for them, but they didn't know it.

"You're alone?" the guitar-case guy asked once more.

"Yeah," she said softly. "But that's not going to matter."

He blinked. All four seemed to have noticed her tone had changed somewhat.

Guitar-case glanced at his partner who'd trailed him off the bus. This second man was a bit heavier and had a thick beard. The two of them took a step towards her now, tense.

"I'm going to say this once," she said conversationally, her tone even.

They took another step towards her.

"If you lay on the ground and interlock your hands behind your heads, I won't hurt you."

The two other men were chuckling now, clearly amused. One had drawn his gun completely, and held it tight, though still pointed at the ground.

They were almost on her now. One was pulling a knife from his hip.

"But if you insist on making this mistake," she continued, "I'm going to hurt you. Badly."

By the time she said Badly, her hand was already moving.

The man with the knife tried to grab her but was stunned to find she was no longer there.

One second, she'd been tottering, pretending as if she had lost her balance, and the next she moved swiftly.

She ducked under his grasping arm, her other hand finding his wrist. She broke it. He screamed in pain as the knife fell.

She caught the knife with her other hand, which she'd already placed under his wrist in anticipation of this.

It wasn't like a dance. And it wasn't like a fistfight. She wasn't a sport fighter or a combat athlete. She had been trained for one thing exactly.

To kill the enemies of her government.

Playing nice with people who fired rockets or shot up bazaars was a good way to end up dead, and so none of her training had been nice.

None of her instincts were either.

She'd been serious when she'd told them to get on the ground.

But now...

They'd made their choice.

Even as the man screamed from his broken wrist, and she caught the knife, she turned towards the man raising his gun.

He shouted, already attempting to pull the trigger.

"Safety," she told him.

The word was a taunt, but also a distraction. He glanced down at his safety, and she flung the knife hilt over blade.

It buried in his chest with a dull thunk.

The man dropped his gun and collapsed before he could get off a shot.

Guitar-case was busily unzipping his bag, reaching for his M4 with desperate motions.

But she was on him, closing the distance again. A long-gun required range. Up close, he didn't stand a chance.

None of them did.

None of them were trained.

She wrapped her arm around his throat, twisting a hand behind his back, pinning it with her knee, and then locking in the choke with her elbow.

She applied steady pressure and he let out short, gasping sounds.

But the breathing eventually stopped. She dropped him unconscious to the ground, and he fell like a marionette with snipped strings, collapsing in an ungraceful pile on the grass darkened by the shadow of the tent.

One man bled with a knife in his chest. Another gripped his broken wrist, moaning. The third lay unconscious on the ground.

The fourth stared at her, gobsmacked and pale.

He looked as if he'd wet himself.

She kept her tone grim and enunciated her words clearly.

"Last chance," she said simply. Even in battle, she preferred short, curt sentences. Words had power, some said—but actions amplified them.

Her voice was like a starter pistol. The man yelped and dropped into a heap on the ground, hands over his head.

He trembled in the grass, face down, eating turf.

She scanned over her fallen foes, bent over, and picked up the handgun. In three swift motions, she unchambered the live round, ejected the mag and disassembled the barrel.

She tossed the pieces in three directions.

She grabbed the Carbine and, careful not to leave a fingerprint, she tossed it far away from the unconscious would-be aggressor.

The older, middle-aged woman was staring, trembling on the ground.

"Do you have any rope?" Anna said conversationally.

"W-what?"

"Rope," she repeated.

"I... I... what... Who are they? Who are you?"

Anna shrugged. "Don't know who they are."

"So... you just... is he dead?" she stared in horror at the man with the knife in his chest.

Anna glanced at the man and frowned. "You can call paramedics. There might be time. I missed his heart."

She spoke matter-of-factly, solving a problem rather than processing an emotion. "Rope?" she repeated, returning to the problem at hand.

"There... there's some spare from putting up the tent. It's..." she pointed with a trembling hand over her shoulder.

Anna approached the woman, who was still sitting in the grass from where she'd been tripped. Anna helped her to her feet, dusting off the woman's fleece.

"Could you please bring me some? I'll keep an eye on them."

"Some what?"

"Rope," Anna said again, her tone even, calm.

Civilians needed calm. It was contagious.

She waited as the woman stumbled off, hastening behind the stage. Anna kept her eye on the man with his hands locked behind his head.

The employee returned a few seconds later, carrying rope.

Anna thanked the woman, then went about the business of tying the men tightly. In the right hands, rope was almost as good as handcuffs. The knot she used was an easy one to untie, but almost impossible to work free if the tied person couldn't use their hands.

When all three men were secured, she turned to the woman.

"Do you have a phone?"

"Y-yes..."

"Call the police."

And then Anna turned to leave.

"Where are you going?" the woman called out.

"Yosemite," she called back.

"You... you can't leave!"

Anna looked at the woman. "I'd rather not talk with the cops."

The employee just gaped at Anna. Her mouth opened, closed, then opened again.

Anna gave a small nod. "They won't be able to hurt you. Just call the cops. Get paramedics. Leave the tent; I'm guessing there's evidence of whatever they were planning on their phones and the cops will sort it out with your testimony." The woman's eyes were beginning to swim as if she might break down, and Anna tilted her head to maintain her gaze. "It'll be fine. You can do this." Anna gave a ghost of a smile, which she hoped was reassuring. And then she turned once more, striding swiftly away.

"Who are you?" the woman called again.

But Anna didn't reply.

A name wouldn't have answered that question.

In fact, Anna had already shown the woman who she was.

The proof lay bleeding in the grass.

She moved swiftly away.

She didn't know what those men had been up to. Didn't know what they'd wanted.

She didn't much care, either.

Men with a plan often thought highly of whatever damage they intended to do. She didn't think of it as anything more than a leaking pipe. Or a broken gutter. She didn't care what type of pipe was leaking, nor the brand name of the gutter. All she cared about was fixing the problem.

And now?

The problem was fixed.

And so on to Yosemite.

As she picked up her pace, she pulled out her own phone. A burner. The third one she'd bought this month. Calling the cops would render it useless to her. She wanted to get another few days of use before disposing of it.

She stared at the message on the screen, though.

A single word.

A word that had prompted her to get on a bus in Ohio and overnight to California.

A word that had brought her home.

It wasn't the word so much as the messenger who'd caught her attention.

She read the message, frowning.

Please help.

She stowed her phone, picked up her pace, and moved swiftly towards the bus stop.

She was going home. For the first time in ten years. Home. No one else could've lured her back. Not her mother... not her childhood friends. Not her nephews or nieces.

But this message could. The person who sent it was the only one.

Please help.

She felt a shiver run down her spine. She noticed the camera over the bus stop and ducked her head, keeping her face from view.

Her C-Class RV would be waiting for her. She'd had a service drop it off in Yosemite—it had taken some doing, seeing as the RV had been in an impound lot in Washington for three months.

Now, though, she was going home.

Her baby sister was in trouble.

Chapter 3

Anna stepped into the diner where she was supposed to meet her sister, feeling her nerves and a pit in her stomach.

She was home.

She glanced at her phone, confirming the date and time once more. Mammoth Lakes was a small, but picturesque town, in the Sierra mountains only a forty-five-minute drive from Yosemite National Park.

She hadn't returned in nearly ten years, but the diner was exactly as she remembered it.

Warm and inviting, with its traditional wood-paneled walls and checkered floor. A jukebox in the corner played old country songs that filled the room with a familiar comfort. The room emanated the smell of coffee and freshly baked pies, making it difficult for Anna to keep her stomach from growling.

At one of the tables in the center of the room sat a group of locals who had been coming to this diner since before Anna was born. They were all dressed in flannel shirts and well-worn jeans, their faces weathered by years spent out in the sun. They spoke in low voices, laughing occasionally at some joke or story being told amongst them.

The windows along one side of the diner overlooked Mammoth Lakes, providing an incredible view of mountains that stretched into eternity. The lake glistened like a diamond beneath a clear blue sky, while puffy white clouds lazily drifted across its surface.

In spite of her nerves, Anna smiled as she looked around her childhood home. It felt nostalgic to be here again after so long away.

Though she hadn't felt this nervous since her first black ops mission.

"Hey there, darling. You're welcome, but the cold ain't."

She glanced towards where a warm-faced woman was standing behind the diner's counter, serving up a fresh plate of steaming hash browns and eggs to an eager customer.

Anna gave a quick, apologetic nod, then hooked the door with her foot behind her, closing it, and shutting off the crisp lake breeze coming in under the afternoon sun.

Instinctively, she noted the three egress points in the diner. Back exit, front door, and a floor-to-ceiling, lake-facing window.

Additionally, she spotted the men, quickly cataloging their positions in the room. She noted an old-timer with an obvious concealed carry and the large set of steak knives directly behind the counter.

All of this information processed rapidly.

Her sister, however, was nowhere to be seen.

She approached the counter, raising a hand in greeting towards the kind-faced cook.

"Anything I can get you, dear? Coffee?"

"No, thanks."

Anna didn't drink caffeine. The first couple of years back as a civilian had been rough. Pain pills and alcohol had been a constant temptation. She found a strict, disciplined diet was the best way to control any such urge.

Sometimes, she felt like a shark. She'd once heard the creatures could never stop moving, or they'd sink to the bottom of the ocean and die.

She had to keep moving, or the darkness would catch up.

"Just water," she said simply.

"Anything to eat?"

"Yeah, but I'll wait."

"Meeting someone, dear?"

Anna just nodded politely. "Yes, ma'am."

The woman brushed some gray hairs from her face and smiled at Anna. She then turned to grab an orange juice and hand it to another customer.

"You look familiar," the woman said as she returned her attention to Anna. "Do I know you?"

Anna didn't recognize this woman, but she did recognize a few of the other figures in the diner. Mammoth Lakes wasn't that large of a town, but the picturesque scenery often invited itinerants or transplants.

She shrugged. "I used to live here."

"Oh? Back on vacation?"

"Something like that." She checked her phone. Here. She'd texted ten minutes ago.

So where was Beth?

It wasn't like her little sister to be late.

Then again... did she even know Beth anymore?

Ten years was a very long time.

The door jangled, and she turned quickly but it was only an older lady and a man with a walker.

She looked back at the cook behind the counter.

"Sorry, dear. But we're getting crowded. Would you care to order something? Just to reserve the spot?"

The woman said it with a wince as if suggesting that she didn't want to make Anna do it, but as if higher powers required this spiel.

Anna just nodded. She pulled out another tenner. "Whatever you recommend," she said. "Keep the change." She added another bill.

Her wallet was still flush. She didn't use plastic cards. Didn't believe in providing name and address to some faceless corporation.

She kept no money in banks, and most of her life savings was in the form of gold bullion hidden in her RV. She didn't even know her social security number.

A life off the books in other countries translated relatively easily to an off-grid life in this one as well.

The woman behind the counter snatched the bills off the marble with a practiced hand, smiled sweetly, then turned to whip up a batch of eggs.

Anna glanced at her phone again.

No text message.

The last message, two days ago, had simply read Please help.

And then, Tina's Diner. Noon.

No other messages. One of only two numbers stored in Anna's phone. Her baby sister... and also Casper. Casper—his call sign from the Seals—was the only team member she kept in contact with. An old friend... She sighed. She didn't have many friends.

GUARDIAN'S VENGEANCE

But of the two numbers stored in her phone, only her sister had messaged her in the last year. So why wasn't she replying *now*?

She frowned, staring at the device.

Here. She texted again, wondering if perhaps the burner had failed to send it the first time.

Her gaze moved to the large window, scanning the parking lot.

But no sign of her sister there, either.

She tried calling.

Straight to voicemail.

The voicemail recording gave her pause. *"I'm sorry, I can't come to the phone right now. Please leave a message."*

She held her phone, staring out the window as her baby sister's sweet voice echoed over the device. Beth was five years younger. She'd only been fifteen when Anna had joined the military, following in her father's footsteps.

Beth had written Anna, every single week though Anna hadn't always been able to access her email. Especially not in mid-mission. Infiltration took time and often required one to leave everything behind to complete the assignment.

But when she returned from a successful op, she would be greeted by a deluge of emails from Beth.

She had pictures of Beth at her wedding. Pictures of Beth's first child. Her second child.

Anna found her throat tightening as emotion welled up within her.

She'd often tried to reply to Beth's emails, but... she never made enough time.

She ran a hand through her hair, letting out a long breath of air.

Beth had been a lifeline. Especially through some of the darker moments...

Anna's mind tried to move back to other memories. Her hand gripped the water glass slick with condensation.

She forced her thoughts back to the present.

"...this morning. Burned to the ground..." Someone was saying from the table next to her.

Anne glanced over.

A man named Henry Titus was talking to an old friend of his. She didn't remember the friend's name, but he went to the same church as Henry. The two men were eating bacon omelets lathered with cheddar cheese, and talking in low, conspiratorial voices.

"And the family was inside?"

"Don't know. God, I hope not," Henry was saying. "Tragic, isn't it? In our town?"

Anna was staring at him now.

She couldn't help but overhear their conversation: a fire had burned down a family's home?

Her heart skipped another beat.

"Where did it happen?" she asked, her voice low and gruff.

The two men at the table turned to look at her, surprised by her sudden interest.

"Huh?" Henry said. "Oh, uh, down on the south side of town. Some kind of electrical fire, I heard."

Anna's mind was racing.

"Do you know the address?"

"Umm... say, do I know you?"

Anna sidestepped the question. She hadn't realized when she'd regained her feet, but she was now standing next to the old-timer, staring at him intently. "What street?"

"I think... Pine?"

Her stomach plummeted.

Her sister lived on Pine. "I need your phone," she said.

The man blinked.

"Please," she added, keeping her emotions in check despite the horror welling within her.

"I'm... I'm sorry. Who are you?"

"I know someone who lives on Pine Street. Please, can I borrow your phone?"

"It's on the TV; just look at the news. All anyone local is talking about," Henry said, waving a ketchup-stained finger toward the small TV mounted on the wall.

Anna's eyes followed his gesture to the TV screen, where a news anchor was reporting on the fire that had burned down a home on Pine Street. The camera panned to show the charred remains of what was once a beautiful house.

Anna stared. She recognized the blue siding and purple shutters—colorful, just like Beth.

She'd never visited the house, before, but had seen plenty of pictures in the emails her baby sister had sent.

And now...

The place was a heaping wreck. Char marks stained the remains of the house, and the roof had caved in. There was no way anyone could have survived that.

Her heart sank as she realized that this was Beth's home. Her sister hadn't shown up.

Please help.

And by the looks of things, Anna had come too damn late.

She shivered, feeling a cold tingling sensation down her spine.

She tried to suppress the rising sense of horror.

She turned to the two men at the table. "I need a ride," she said simply.

The men shared a look.

"I can pay."

But Henry, the churchgoing man, gave a long sigh and pushed to his feet. "You know who's house that is?" he said grimly.

Her voice was a mask, betraying no emotion as she replied. "My sister's."

The man stared at her. "Shit..." Then he crossed himself. "Don't gotta pay. Work's that way for me anyhow. Come on. Got a name?"

"Anna," she said quietly.

"Anna?" He shot her a glance and hesitated, studying her. Then he shook his head.

She didn't help him try and place her face.

Her family's name was associated with tragedy. After what had happened to her father... After her mother had disowned her...

And now this?

She felt that same icy, tingling sensation, and she could feel her heart pounding as she followed Henry from the diner.

"Ma'am, your lunch!" called the cook's voice.

"Give it to someone else," she called back. "Thanks," she added.

It didn't cost anything to be polite, and sometimes, routine and regularity could help stem the tide of rising emotions.

She could feel panic clawing its way in, terror in her chest.

But she breathed in, out.

Back in SEAL school, one had to narrow their focus. One step at a time. One step, then another. Small, immediate commitments led to endurance.

She couldn't think a mile down the road. She had to focus on the next step.

"Pine street?" Henry asked as he slipped into his old, rusted truck, and pushed open the door for her to join him.

"Yes," she said quietly.

He shot her a sidelong glance. "Alrighty."

He put the car in gear.

Inside, the truck smelled of cigarette smoke and old leather. Anna tried to focus on her breathing, to center herself. Henry drove in silence, and Anna was grateful for it. She just wanted to get there as soon as possible.

When they finally arrived, the sight of the house made Anna's heart drop into her stomach. The structure was in ruins, barely standing, and firefighters were still dousing the smoldering remains with water.

She stared in shock. Seeing it on the television, it hadn't felt real.

But now...

Henry pulled the truck to a stop and turned to look at her. "I'm sorry," he said gruffly.

Anna nodded, unable to speak. All she could do was stare at the remains of the house.

After a few moments, she forced herself to get out of the truck. She slid a handful of tenners across the seat.

He pushed them back into her hand.

"Keep it," he said.

"I insist," she said.

"No. Keep it. I mean it. Don't need it." Henry watched her as she shut the door, and nodded her thanks. He then began rolling away.

She turned away from Henry. She knew that she had to do something: she couldn't just stand there and grieve. She had to find out what had happened.

She walked up to one of the firefighters. "Excuse me," she said, her voice shaking. "Do you know if anyone was inside?"

The firefighter turned to her, his face grim. "I'm sorry, ma'am," he said. "We found two bodies inside. We're still waiting on identification..."

"Kids?" Anna said, her voice as cold as she felt.

"I... do you know the people here?"

"My sister," she said simply.

The firefighter blinked. "Anna?" he said, his voice in shock.

She stared at the firefighter, a young man, perhaps in his late twenties.

"Carter?" she said, frowning. "Football?"

"Lacrosse," he replied. "I was two years below you in high school. Holy... I—" Carter's mouth flapped as he quickly swallowed what he'd been about to say and backtracked, wiping soot from his face.

Suddenly Anna remembered exactly why the firefighter's face danced at the edge of recognition. Memories of a less-than-subtle, teenage crush that a high-school-aged Carter had carried for her returned in waves of vague impressions and half-remembered thoughts.

"Sorry," said Carter with a sigh. "Been a really long day. Up since three." His fingers left dark streaks along his face.

Anna didn't take offense. Instead, she spotted an opportunity. Every resource could be used. As the saying went, one had to use every part of the buffalo. And an old, high school crush from someone she scarcely remembered? It felt callous, but she was far beyond any of that right now.

"Can I look around?" she said simply.

He looked uncomfortable. "I... I don't think I can let you do that. It's still burning in parts. The place is sealed off."

"Please?" she said.

He sighed, rubbing his hand through his hair again. "You're military, right?"

"Something like that," she said.

She could tell he'd been hoping for some rank or job he could use as an excuse to let her through. Carter shot another look over his shoulder. A few other firefighters were dragging a hose back to their truck. Police cars were lining the street, at a safe distance.

He hesitated. "I mean... I really can't bring you in."

"Fine. Just don't stop me," she said simply. And she began to walk towards the burnt building, feeling like a ghost approaching familiar shores.

Carter just stared after her; she could feel his eyes on her.

But he didn't call out.

She slipped along behind the nearby unit. Another house, smaller and older... But still standing, though the west-facing facade was scorched.

Then, no longer in view of the street, standing in the alley between the two homes, Anna made her way toward the charred remains of her sister's house. She felt a lump form in her throat as she approached the side door. The wood was missing, leaving only the metal frame behind.

Checking to make sure the structure above her was sound, she then took a deep breath and stepped inside. The smell of smoke and ash was overpowering. The entire interior was blackened and burnt. It was a miracle that the whole house hadn't collapsed yet. Anna made her way towards the charred remains of the house. She felt a lump form in her throat as she approached the front door.

Then, she heard a footstep. A voice.

"What the hell do you think you're doing in here?" the voice demanded.

She tensed and turned slowly to find herself facing an angry face and the barrel of a gun.

Chapter 4

Anna turned slowly, raising her hands, her feet scuffing against the charred linoleum which had bubbled like burnt caramel.

A man was standing in the rubble, gun in hand, eyes narrowed. She analyzed the threat as quick as thought.

Six foot three. Well-built. Coroner's outfit, which consisted of a lab coat and slacks now stained with soot. He had on blue crime scene gloves and plastic wraps over his shoes. The gun was a Glock, held with a practiced ease that told her the man had used it before.

He glared at her, his hands steady.

She didn't speak at first, but after assessing the threat, and glancing past the man in the coroner's outfit, she said, "I'm the sister of the home owner."

The man hesitated, still frowning.

She kept her own hands spread, showing that she was unarmed.

"Who let you in here?" he demanded. "This is an active crime scene."

"I'm here to confirm the identity of the deceased," she said. This was true. No one had technically given her permission to do so, but it was still an accurate statement.

The coroner paused.

"Might make your job easier," she added.

"And who authorized this?"

Under this deluge of questions, she felt herself only conceding ground. So instead, she pointed at his weapon. "Do coroners normally carry?"

"In a double homicide scene, this coroner does," he shot back.

"Where are the bodies?"

Her eyes moved past him, and she spotted a white tarp in the adjoining room, through a burnt doorway.

She went still. She could make out the figures of two forms under the tarp.

She moved towards it.

"Hey. Hey!" he said, his voice rising in volume. He kept his gun on her.

She brushed past him, giving him a wide enough berth that he wouldn't consider her a threat.

"I said stop!" he demanded.

"Shoot me then," she muttered.

She approached the tarp with the bodies, ignoring the coroner now.

"Have you identified them?" she said quietly.

The coroner just gaped at her, looking flustered. He wore glasses that had fogged up, either from the cool air or the lingering steam and ash. His features were taut, both due to the tense situation, and also an impressively low bodyfat percentage. She supposed he was likely a runner of some sort.

She also liked to run, though her workouts were... a bit more intense than most were accustomed too.

She realized her mind was processing the mundane, trying to flee the real reason she was standing in front of the tarp.

Her mind simply didn't want to go there.

But she knew she couldn't avoid it for much longer.

And soon, the coroner would start calling for backup.

"I'll be out of your hair," she said, her voice numb. "Just one second."

She reached down, careful not to disturb evidence or muss the crime scene as she pulled the tarp aside, revealing two, badly burnt bodies.

They were blackened beyond recognition.

Anna's stomach lurched at the sight. She could barely keep herself from retching. She had seen plenty of dead bodies in her line of work, but this was different. It was personal. She knew who these people were. They were her family.

Anna felt a wave of nausea wash over her. This was the moment she had been dreading since she first learned about the fire. She had hoped against hope that it was all a mistake, that her sister and brother-in-law had somehow escaped the inferno. But now, as she stared down at the charred remains... the hope was rapidly depleting.

She took a deep breath, willing herself to stay focused. She was here for a reason, and she couldn't let her emotions get in the way. She scanned the bodies, looking for any marks or tattoos that might help her identify them.

But the skin was so badly burned, there were no significant marks.

"Did you know these men?" the coroner said reluctantly.

He still hadn't called for help, but she noticed how his hand was pressing a button on a radio at his hip.

Backup would be coming shortly.

"Men?" she said, feeling a flicker of emotion.

"Yes. They're both men."

She turned sharply, staring at the coroner. "You're certain?"

"Yes," he said, eyes narrowing. "Do you know them?"

Her heart was pounding now. "Were any children discovered?" she asked.

"No. Just these two."

Her mind shifted to her sister. To her nephew and niece. Her brother-in-law was a shorter man.

Both these men were well over six foot, even burnt.

Now, as she allowed the emotions of horror to slip away, she focused on the bodies. Really seeing them.

This wasn't her family.

A flicker of hope sparked in her chest.

The coroner was still holding her at gunpoint.

But now, as relief flooded her, washing through her like a tidal wave, she found herself paying much closer attention to the man with the Glock.

"Why haven't you called for backup," she said quietly.

His hand was still on the radio, but now, she could see that the toggle switch for power was off.

He blinked. "You need to leave, now."

She turned to face him fully. The scent of ash still lingered in the house, swirling about. She could feel her eyes beginning to water from the horrible air quality.

"Why haven't you called for backup?" she repeated, more firmly.

Now, suspicion was slowly dawning on her.

She'd been able to sneak into the burnt house... The cops outside were still securing the area. The firefighters had only just started to pull back their trucks.

The area would have to be declared safe before a coroner was allowed on scene.

The man wore booties and gloves. He wore a white jacket... But no identification. He wasn't calling for backup. And he held a gun.

He wanted her to leave. But she was dressed in a wind-breaker and black slacks. She could easily have been construed as an off-duty officer called to the scene.

Was it normal for a coroner to instantly pull a gun?

No... No, it wasn't normal at all.

"You're not the coroner," she said quietly, her eyes narrowing to slits.

The man with the gun stared at her, hesitant.

She made a move toward him, but then he cursed, turned on his heel, and sprinted away.

She didn't hesitate. She sprinted after the strange gunman as he raced through the burnt house, toward the back door. His gun was tossed to the side. And as it landed it didn't clatter so much as crack.

A plastic toy.

He'd been pointing a plastic toy at her. She felt a flash of shame. Stupid... she'd thought her sister was dead. She'd been distracted. And he'd been holding the fake gun in such a way to conceal it for the most part, but she should've known.

Now, though, he sprinted down a hall, leaving swirls of ash behind him.

He cursed as his foot shattered through a hollowed-out floorboard. He yanked it free and continued sprinting.

She chased after him, leaping over the broken section of floor.

He threw himself through a door and into a living room. She followed, taking in the details of the destroyed room; burnt curtains, broken furniture, shattered glass.

The man stumbled over a chair as he tried to make his escape. He scrambled over it and lunged towards the window. But she was too fast; she grabbed his leg and yanked him back. He kicked free of her grip and stumbled to the other side of the table.

Now, a glass window prevented further escape—the glass was smudged and streaked with ash.

The man with the glasses shot a panicked look toward her. Hesitated only a moment, and as she lunged at him again, he cursed and flung himself bodily through the window with a loud crash.

GUARDIAN'S VENGEANCE

Glass shattered, falling in shards as the man went through the window. Anna stared after the man, taking in the sight of broken glass and the ash-covered curtains.

She could see him running towards the forest fringe.

She hesitated only briefly, staring at the jagged pieces of glass in the frame, jutting out like a monster's gnawing teeth.

She cursed, braced her arm, and cleared as much of the debris as possible. Then, with a running start, she flung herself like a diver through the window.

She hit the grass, rolled, and regained her feet.

Bright flashing lights reflected off the windows of the neighbor's house as she tore through the backyard in pursuit of the fleeing man.

Who was this?

Was he involved?

The two victims in the house were too tall. Neither of them could've been her sister's family members.

She needed answers. Propelled by a wave of relief for her sister and fueled by a desperate need for answers, she ran after him, determined to catch up before he disappeared completely.

The man was fast, and he kept glancing over his shoulder as he navigated the wooded lot behind the house.

Mammoth Lakes was a picturesque town, but the surrounding woods and rising slopes leading to the mountain made the terrain difficult to navigate.

But in a test of endurance?

She wasn't going to lose.

She could already see the man flagging ahead of her.

He was slowing a bit, but still pushing gamely on, to his credit.

Her lungs were burning from the dead sprint. Her arms and legs were like pistons, but her muscles twinged and her body ached from the jarring steps against the ground. She felt blood along her forearm where a piece of glass from the shattered window had exacted its vengeance.

But all of this she ignored.

Ahead, she spotted a tree.

Keep sprinting until the tree, she told herself.

And that was all that mattered.

GUARDIAN'S VENGEANCE

She didn't look past the tree. She didn't think what came next. When her mind tried to veer off, she kept it on track.

She reached the tree.

Keep sprinting until that stone.

Another arbitrary line.

She could give up. She could quit. Once a commitment was done, she allowed herself permission to stop. But only if her will failed.

And it didn't.

She now reached the stone, still at a dead sprint. Her body protested, and ached, but her mind had always been stronger than her body.

Her will had always been able to control her desire for rest.

The man ahead of her was definitely slowing now. His hand kept darting to his flank, and she could hear him wheezing and gasping, his breath rising like plumes above him under the noon sun.

They reached an incline, in the woods, leading up the slope of the mountain base.

The man stumbled.

She kept coming.

He looked back at her, and his eyes widened briefly behind his glasses. Stunned to see her still closing the distance.

He tried to rise, but his legs buckled under him.

And then she was on him.

She tackled him to the ground as he tried to rise again. They both hit the leaves with a dull thump, and the breath whooshed from her lungs—what little breath remained.

The man tried vainly to put up a bit of a fight, but he was so exhausted, so gassed, that he could barely breath under her.

She used this to her advantage, putting her full weight on his chest, compressing his lungs further.

He wheezed, desperate.

"Stop fighting!" she commanded.

He reluctantly lowered his hands from where they'd been scrambling at her fingers.

She made sure he was unarmed, patting him down where he lay in the leaves. When he struggled, she increased the pressure on his chest.

GUARDIAN'S VENGEANCE

But he didn't seem to have much energy left for fighting, as all his attention was on breathing.

"You're fast," he muttered.

She blinked. A strange comment. Almost as if the man were amused despite his pain.

Her palms struck something tiny and solid in the man's pocket. No, several small items from the way they clacked together. A small ball of indignation tightened in her chest as she realized what they were, but now certain that he wasn't carrying any weapons, she tugged him to his feet.

"These don't match your complexion," she muttered, pulling the small bag from his pocket and holding it between them.

The man winced, staring at the items.

Earrings and necklaces.

"Was this why you were in my sister's house?" she demanded. "Stealing?"

He just grimaced and shook his head.

She scowled at him, still holding the little bag of jewelry. Then she shoved him.

He stumbled forward.

"Walk!" she commanded.

"W-where are we going?"

"Someplace private," she said, her voice cold. "We need to have a little chat."

Chapter 5

Anna pushed the man ahead of her, muttering, "Keep quiet."

Her voice carried the threat.

He stumbled forward, no longer breathing heavily. Anna's RV had been brought from the impound lot to a campsite only twenty minutes from her sister's house, and the man hadn't said a word in their entire hike to it.

Now, as Anna approached her RV, her hand still pushing against her captive's back, she felt a wave of nostalgia.

It was a strange thing to have a home on wheels, but she found herself smiling as she drew near.

"Wh-what are you going to do with me?" the man said, his voice shaking.

He'd clearly thought she was going to take him to the police but now that they were here, she could feel the fear emanating from him as he no doubt recalled every true crime story he'd ever heard about murderers leading someone into the woods to kill them.

The campsite was isolated, just as she'd requested from the contact whom she'd paid to deliver her RV the previous week. The trees around them blocked the view from the surrounding area and provided the perfect amount of privacy.

Anna ignored the man's question, shoving him towards the RV's door. The branches swayed in the breeze, and the only other sound was the occasional chirp of a bird.

Home sweet home.

The RV itself had more than one scratch mark on its beige surface. The logo of the company that had made the mobile home had long since faded off, leaving only a few letters behind. With their former companions faded off, the oddly spaced characters now seemed to spell out the word Hound.

Though the n was supposed to be an m, she thought. She'd purchased the RV third-hand, after all.

"Get in," she commanded tersely.

He hesitated before complying.

Once inside, Anna gestured for him to take a seat at the tiny kitchen table. She crossed her arms and stared at him, her eyes icy.

"I want to know why you were in my sister's house." Her voice was low and controlled.

The man swallowed, then shook his head. He reached up, adjusting his glasses and placing them on the table.

It was only now that she realized the glass didn't magnify the wood grain. She picked up his glasses, frowning. "These aren't even real, are they?"

He shrugged sheepishly, rubbing at the back of his head. "Er... fashion statement?"

"You think you're funny?"

"No. Definitely not."

She tossed the small bag of jewelry on the table. "What's this?"

"A bag," he said.

She studied him for a moment. "I'm going to need you to stop being a wise-ass."

"Huh. Won't be easy," he quipped.

He was about to add more but grunted instead as she drove the heel of her palm into his face. His head snapped back, and blood almost instantly welled from his left nostril.

"That was a heel strike to cartilage," she said conversationally, as he groaned, clutching at his bleeding nose. "If I'd hit harder, it would've shattered your nasal canal. So... less lip, okay?"

He grimaced, dabbing at his nose, but nodding gingerly.

His hair was wild and unkempt. Dark strands fell in a tangle over his emerald eyes. He shifted nervously in the chair, blowing air to fluff his hair from his eyes.

"I... I just wanted to make a quick buck," he said hurriedly. "Really... I... My family is struggling. I didn't know anyone was dead. I swear. I just heard about the house being burnt."

"How?"

"My brother's a firefighter," he said urgently. He was shaking his head now, his lower lip trembling.

As he talked, she reached into his pocket and pulled out his cellphone. He grimaced but allowed her to use his finger to open the biometric lock.

He was saying, "I... I didn't know where else to go. I thought I could take a couple of things and sell them at a pawn shop.

I really..." he swallowed. "Didn't want to. But... but I'm out of work. My kids have been eating watered-down soup. For like two weeks! I'm sorry." His voice was cracking now. A single tear seemed to appear in one of those emerald eyes.

He looked embarrassed, ashamed.

"I didn't know," he sobbed. "I'm so... sorry."

"Waldo?" she said. "Really? You've saved your name in the phone as Waldo? Like as in where's waldo?"

He wrinkled his nose. "Family name."

"Waldo Strange?"

She looked up at him, quirking an eyebrow.

He shifted uncomfortably. "The Third."

"Waldo Strange the Third? Bullshit."

"Not even!" he said. Then his hand darted up to protect his nose.

She had entered the name into a web search and pressed enter.

As the page loaded, Waldo Strange the Third was pulling on her heartstrings some more. "I know I shouldn't have. I've never done anything like this before, but little Gracie... she's only four.

Her birthday is next week, and she's already gone two years without any presents, and so I just—"

She punched him in the nose again. His head snapped back, and now blood was trickling from both nostrils.

"What the hell!" he yelled, his voice nasally.

"Asshole," she said, turning the phone towards him.

A slew of courtroom reports described the various and multiple burglaries that Waldo Strange the Third had been indicted for over the years. By the looks of things, he'd been in and out of prison for nearly a decade and a half, since he'd been a teenager.

Waldo shifted sheepishly. "Ah... yeh, well... Shit."

He brightened up suddenly, and his voice no longer warbled. The tears were gone from his eyes, and now, despite his bloody nose, he was smiling at her with the biggest, shit-eating grin she'd ever seen.

"Can't blame a guy for trying, huh?"

"Last chance," she said, "What were you doing in my sister's house?"

"Purloining. Pinching. Knicking knacks."

She raised her hand.

"Stealing!" he yelped. "I was stealing!"

"Do you ever just answer a question straight?" she snapped.

He shook his head and crossed his heart. "Trying my best, but I've got a condition."

"Stupid isn't a condition. In your case, it's a choice."

"Funny." He winked, leaning back in the chair now, and looking relaxed all of a sudden. "But no. I'm ataraxic."

"You're an asshole."

"So you've said, but really. I've got a doctor's note and everything."

She sighed, feeling weary now. Her worry for her sister continued to mount. And her irritation at Waldo Strange the Third was only growing. "Ataraxic. What's that, like some kind of kleptomania or something?"

"Means I don't feel fear," he said quickly. "Or anxiety. I don't have..." he wrinkled his nose, then winced and dropped the expression. "Doc said I don't have a proportional response to human stressors. You ever see that documentary about the climber who scaled a cliff with no ropes? I've got that thing."

"Ataraxic?" she asked.

"Mhmm, yeah." He shrugged. "Not trying to piss you off... But, I just don't feel fear the normal usual way."

"You lie a lot, don't you?"

"Absolutely. But not about that. I swear I didn't hurt your sister. And those two blokes in the house were men. I'd stake anything on it."

"Your life?" she asked quietly.

He grimaced and swallowed. "Point taken. But I didn't hurt them. Or anyone."

"Tell me how you snuck into my sister's house. What did you see when you arrived?" she said, watching him closely. She would gather as much information via news and police radio once the scene was processed. Now, she knew it was a race against time.

The sad truth of the matter was that most people who went missing never turned up again if gone for more than forty-eight hours.

And as much as she was trying to keep her calm, trying to allow a dispassionate examination of the evidence, Waldo Strange was really starting to get under her skin.

He seemed to sense her rising irritation, because he quickly said, "I was talking to a couple of cop buddies."

"Also friends of your brother?"

"Don't have a brother. Lied about that."

She glared, but he only chortled and continued, shifting about in his seat now and gesticulating like an actor on stage getting into his monologue. "They told me about the burnt house. Told me firefighters were on their way. Neighborhood is a nice one. Real nice, if you know what I mean."

"How could I possibly not know what the words real nice mean?"

"Fair point, well made. But look, I showed up after the place was burnt. Real early. Firefighters were finishing up, and no one questions a man in blue booties." He held up a finger. "That's a life motto to live by. You're welcome."

She massaged the bridge of her nose, her hand clenching into a fist.

"I can prove it!" he said quickly, noticing the gesture.

She frowned at him. "How?"

"Neighbors had a security camera. I disabled it before going in. You can see all the footage beforehand, and up to. I arrived at Eight AM. Well after the house was burned."

She paused, hesitant, studying the man. He was clearly a liar, but he seemed a cheeky, cheerful liar. She'd known men like this before. Usually, they worked for intelligence agencies. He seemed harmless enough. Who carries a plastic gun?

But he'd been at the scene of the crime.

"Did you see anything else?" she said, insistently.

"Nothing," he said.

"Think."

"I..." he trailed off.

She pointed at him. "That. What did you just remember?"

He paused, hesitant. Was he about to feed her more lies? She was going to verify his claim about the security camera, but if he was telling the truth, the clock was already ticking.

He swallowed briefly, then said, "I... I may have been wrong, but there was an unmarked vehicle at the scene. When I first arrived. It wasn't there later."

"Unmarked? So you think they were cops?"

"Had to be," he said.

"What made you think that?"

"They had a certain look to them. Like they were used to being in charge. I could tell they weren't normal folks."

"Normal like you?"

"Fair point, well made," he said, repeating the strange phrase. But he shrugged. "I dunno... Haven't seen them around before. But... I'm relatively new to the area."

"Shocking to think you'd have to move a lot," she said sarcastically, then sighed. "Did you see a license plate?"

"Nope."

He held up a finger. "But it was parked near that security camera I mentioned."

She nodded slowly. "And it was gone before the investigation was over?"

"Yeah, that's the strange part. it was there, then left before the firefighters had even cleared the house." He flashed her a car salesman smile, watching her earnestly.

She glared back at him.

"You have lovely teeth, did you know that?" he said.

She pushed him and he toppled over backwards in his chair. To his credit, he groaned but remained on the ground as she moved towards the front of the RV.

"Stay down," she called over her shoulder.

The more time she spent with this guy, the less of a threat he seemed.

He didn't strike her as the violent sort. An asshole? Yes.

But an arsonist asshole?

Perhaps not.

Which meant her sister was somewhere else... Her sister's family was... in danger? In hiding?

The text message had simply read Please help.

She grit her teeth, sliding into the driver's side of her RV and putting the vehicle into gear.

She shot a quick glance in the rearview mirror to make sure Waldo was still on the ground. He nursed his nose, but she noticed him tracing a smiley face on the floor in his own blood.

She shook her head.

He was like a child... not a killer. But she'd seen killers come in all shapes and sizes. She watched in the mirror as he drew a couple of phallic shapes in crimson, chuckling at his cleverness.

Ataraxic... she'd never heard of the condition before. An inability to feel fear?

He was either telling the truth, or he had an excellent poker face.

She pulled out of the camping spot, grateful to feel the familiar rumble of her vehicle's engine as she backed up.

"Where?" she called over her shoulder.

"Er, sorry, what's that?"

"Where's this house with the security camera."

"Oh... yeah. Pine street. I can point it out. Mind if I get up?"

"Stay down."

"Sure thing."

She caught him flashing her the bird in the mirror, but her worries on behalf of her sister were only rising, and she floored the gas pedal, peeling out of the campsite in a cloud of dust.

Chapter 6

The cold metal of the gun barrel pressed against Beth's temple as she stood in the darkness, shivering. Her husband, Tom, clutched their two children close to his chest, trying to shield them from the chilling rain and the horrors unfolding before them. Little Tony was only five, and Sarah, barely three, yet they were being ushered into the back of a large, rusty truck at gunpoint—a monstrous vehicle that seemed to swallow all light with its dark silhouette.

"Get in!" the gruff voice demanded again, making Beth flinch. She watched as her husband jolted towards the back of the truck with their children, their tiny faces etched with fear and confusion.

"Mommy!" Sarah cried out, reaching for her mother. Beth tried to smile reassuringly while forcing back hot tears.

"Shh, it's okay, baby," she whispered, hoisting herself up into the dark void. As her feet left the wet gravel, she felt her world slipping away, replaced by an overwhelming sense of dread.

The air coming from the truck was thick with the scent of rust and stale sweat. Beth strained her eyes, desperate to make out any detail that might help them escape this nightmare. She thought of her sister, Anna, and how she seemed to have a plan for everything. What would Anna do? What would Anna do? The thoughts echoed in Beth's mind, and she bit her lip, wincing against the pain. She shared the same green eyes as her sister, and a similar, upturned nose. But her hair was blonde, and her features, quite unlike her sister's, were streaked with makeup. Her thoughts were a whirlwind, crashing against each other in chaos.

"Keep them quiet," the gunman ordered, his voice muffled beneath a black ski mask. "And maybe you'll live through this."

"Please, don't hurt my family," Tom pleaded, his voice cracking. He held Tony and Sarah tighter, as if he could protect them with his sheer physical form. But Tom wasn't a very large man. He was kind, and he was gentle and he was smart. These were the qualities that had first drawn Beth to him.

"Mommy, I'm scared," their son whimpered, burying his face in his father's coat.

"Me too," Sarah echoed, her tiny voice barely audible.

"Stay close," Beth whispered, her heart threatening to burst out of her chest. "We'll get through this." Her hand rested on the shoulder of her daughter, whose face poked over Tom's shoulder where he cradled both his children—one in each arm.

Two other gunmen were standing behind them on the road, speaking to someone in the Jeep who'd driven them here. The gunmen's voices echoed around them, speaking a language she couldn't recognize. She tried to keep her breathing steady and focused on the task at hand: figuring out what these men wanted and how to get her family out of this alive. What would Anna do? The mantra kept repeating in her mind.

"Move!" one of the masked men barked at the whimpering children, his tone harsh and unforgiving.

"Please, don't talk to them like that," she pleaded, her own voice trembling as she spoke. "They're just scared."

"Shut up!" the gunman snapped in English, glaring at her. His voice was heavily accented.

"Mommy..." Sarah whispered, her eyes filling with tears. "I want to go home."

"Me too, sweetheart," Beth murmured, stroking her daughter's hair. "We'll find a way out of this, I promise."

One of the gunmen roughly grabbed Sarah by the arm, yanking her away from Beth. The child cried out in pain, and Tom instinctively lunged forward to free her from the man's grasp.

"Leave her alone!" he growled, placing his son on the ground, then trying to wrestle his daughter away from the assailant.

"Tom, no!" Beth cried, panic rising in her chest as two other gunmen rushed to restrain him. They brutally beat Tom, fists flying and connecting with sickening thuds. Her husband's anguished cries filled the night air, mingling with the terrified sobs of their children.

"Stop it, please!" Beth screamed, desperate to intervene but held back by the first gunman. "You're hurting him! Just let us go!"

Tom was left gasping for breath on the forest floor behind the truck, blood oozing from his split lip and bruises already forming on his face.

With her heart pounding in her chest, Beth's eyes darted between her husband, who was barely conscious on the ground, and their frightened children huddling together. She knew she had to do something, anything, to protect them.

"Please," she choked out, tears streaming down her face as she threw herself onto Tom's battered body. "He won't do it again. Just let us go. We won't tell anyone, I promise!"

Her hands shook as she tried to shield her husband from further harm. The gunmen exchanged glances before one of them, his eyes cold and unfeeling, pointed his weapon directly at Beth's head.

"Get off him," he snarled.

Beth's breath hitched in her throat, the cold metal of the gun pressing against her temple. Her pulse raced, every instinct screaming for her to fight back, but she quelled the urge, knowing that any resistance would only result in more violence.

"Please," she whispered, tears streaming down her cheeks. "Don't hurt my family."

The gunman's finger twitched on the trigger, and for a split second, Beth saw her life flash before her eyes—her childhood with Anna, their laughter and shared secrets; the love she'd found with Tom; the joy of bringing their children into the world. And now, all of it teetered on the brink of annihilation.

As the barrel of the gun loomed menacingly before her, Beth couldn't help but tremble, knowing that any moment could be her last. The gunman's eyes seemed lifeless, devoid of any emotion or empathy. She tried to make sense of the situation, wondering what possible sin she had committed to warrant such brutal treatment.

"Get up!" the gunman shouted, his voice muffled by the mask he wore. Beth hesitated for a moment, her gaze still locked on the weapon pointed at her head. But then, from the corner of her eye, she noticed something strange—a figure emerging from the shadows.

The others all went quiet, the thugs staring or shifting uncomfortably as the mysterious man came into focus.

He strode towards them, slowly, as if he were simply out for a walk in the park. He was an albino, with a tailored suit hugging his slender frame. His pure white hair fell like snow around his shoulders, and his pink eyes seemed to pierce through the darkness, injecting a chilling air of menace.

"Enough," the albino man commanded, his voice calm yet authoritative. He approached the gunman aiming at Beth, his eyes never leaving the weapon. "Lower your gun."

The albino's demeanor was unnervingly calm, his confidence sending chills down Beth's spine. There was something frightening about the way he carried himself, as though he were fully in control of the situation.

"Put it down," the albino repeated, his tone unchanged. The gunman hesitated for a moment, then finally glanced over at the new arrival. He tensed, freezing in place and letting out a slow, leaking breath. Then, he reluctantly lowered his weapon, releasing a deep breath as he did so. Beth, too, felt her heart rate slowing down, though she remained on high alert.

"Good," the albino said, his pink eyes narrowing as he surveyed the scene. "Now let's get this over with."

The albino's piercing pink eyes locked onto the gunman who had just lowered his weapon. She felt a shiver run down her spine, her fear of the unknown man growing with each passing second. As if sensing her unease, the albino turned to face her and offered a reassuring smile that chilled her to the bone.

"I... sorry," whispered the gunman, his accented voice shaking. "I... didn't know..." he struggled to find the words.

"That it was me?" the albino said. "Yes, yes. I know." He patted the man gently on the shoulder. "I understand." Then, without warning, he whirled around and swiftly drew something from within his suit sleeve with a flash of silver.

The albino slashed the blade across the terrified gunman's throat. Blood sprayed through the air, splattering across the ground like gruesome raindrops. The gunman's eyes bulged in shock, his hands reaching for his gushing wound as he collapsed to the floor, gasping for breath.

The albino ignored the dying croaks of the man, wiping the bloodied knife on the man's mask, leaving a crimson smear across the fabric. He then turned his attention to two other gunmen, who stood frozen in horror, their weapons shaking in their trembling hands.

He spoke in a harsh, grating language, issuing a slew of instructions.

"Y-yes, sir," one of the gunmen stuttered, stumbling over his words as he and his companion hastily moved to obey, dragging the lifeless body away.

As the two remaining thugs exchanged nervous glances, the albino walked toward Beth, his gaze never leaving hers. She fought the urge to tremble under his scrutiny, knowing that showing fear would only make her more vulnerable.

"Such a waste," he mused, his voice deceptively soft. "But I suppose it had to be done."

Beth swallowed hard, forcing herself to maintain eye contact. "P-please just let us go..." she whispered, her voice quivering despite her best efforts.

"Sometimes," the albino replied, his eyes narrowing as he studied her, "a display of power is necessary to keep order."

The albino's pale pink eyes seemed to pierce straight through Beth as if he could discern her every thought and feeling. She shuddered involuntarily, trying to keep herself together in the face of this eerie, unsettling presence.

"Come," he said softly, a smile playing on his lips as he gestured toward the front of the truck. "You'll ride with me."

Beth felt her heart drop like a stone in her chest. The idea of being separated from her family, even for a moment, filled her with an unspeakable dread.

"Please," she whispered, her voice barely audible even to herself. "I can't leave them."

The albino tilted his head, regarding her with an almost curious expression. "I'm not asking," he replied, his tone cool and detached. "Now, come along."

"Please, don't take me away from my children," Beth begged, tears streaming down her cheeks. She glanced at her husband, who lay unconscious on the ground, then at her two young children, their faces streaked with dirt and tears.

"Mommy," her five-year-old son whimpered, reaching out for her.

"Ah, such a touching display," the albino remarked, that same unnerving smile never leaving his face. "But it won't do you any good."

"Please," Beth choked out again, her hands shaking as she clutched at her children. "Don't do this."

"Enough!" the albino snapped, his patience evidently wearing thin. He grabbed her arm, pulling her away from her family with surprising strength. Her children cried out in fear, but there was nothing she could do.

As she stumbled forward, Beth's mind raced, searching desperately for any possible way out of this nightmare. What would Anna do?

As they approached the truck, Beth felt the rough fabric of her sweater beneath her fingertips and seized upon an idea. With a subtle movement, she began to tear the buttons from her sweater, letting them fall to the ground as inconspicuously as possible.

"Get in!" the albino barked, his pink eyes narrowed with impatience. Beth hesitated for a moment, her fingers trembling as she fumbled with the last button, her mind racing with a thousand different scenarios of what might happen next.

The final button dropped from her fingertips, squelching into the mud as she was dragged along the side of the truck and shoved towards the open front passenger door. Harsh lights illuminated the rain-speckled road. A mountain loomed in the distance, casting a long shadow that swallowed the ground.

"Look what you've done," the albino suddenly hissed. She turned sharply and froze in horror. He was crouched like some gargoyle, fingers scraping through the mud. He picked up one, two. He straightened slowly, adjusting his suit with his non-muddied hand. His pink eyes bored into hers as he held up one of the buttons she had torn from her sweater.

"Please..." Beth whispered, her pulse racing. "It was just... I didn't mean—"

"Swallow it," the albino commanded, his voice devoid of emotion. He pressed the cold plastic button against her quivering lips.

Horror swelled within her, but his fingers tapped the button against her lips.

"Now!" he said. His voice was firm, commanding, but still in control.

Again, he had her children. Her husband. She trembled, nodding and opening her mouth. As the tasteless disk slid down her throat, a feeling of helplessness washed over her, drowning any semblance of hope she'd clung to.

"Remember this moment," the albino murmured, his breath hot on her neck. "You're completely isolated now. No one will find you or your family."

Beth fought back tears, refusing to give him the satisfaction of seeing her broken.

Her eyes skimmed across the muddy ground...

She spotted something.

There, near the grass where they'd first left the jeep, where her daughter was standing...

Tony was leaning near his sister, whispering something in her ear. Her son had noticed what she'd been doing. A bright boy, smart. Just like his father.

And she noticed now that Tony had a button of his own. He'd copied his mother.

She watched, stunned as her boy dropped the button on the grass when no one was looking. He kept his eyes downcast and didn't look up.

She felt a jolt of fear. But again, the button went unnoticed.

Suddenly, she was shoved into the cabin. She was forced to step up, her throat sore from swallowing the plastic. She stumbled, but the albino caught her, pushing her into the middle seat. Beth shivered as the truck came to life and the grumbling engine shook the cabin. Another man in a ski mask sat in the front, and she glanced in the mirrors only to find the gunman the albino had killed already removed.

Her family was also gone, but she could hear them crying in the back compartment of the cargo hauler.

They were still alive.

For now.

She let out a faint whimper and felt the albino clutch her wrist.

"None of that now," he whispered, his voice rasping. "This has only just started. Save your energy."

She sat between the masked man and the albino, trembling horribly as the truck started to move, turning onto the main road and picking up speed as it raced away into the pelting of a rainstorm.

Chapter 7

Anna leaned against the side of her RV, listening to the raindrops pattering against the roof.

Her clothing was damp now, and rain slipped down her bangs, trembling on the edge of her white shock of hair, and fell past her chin towards the ground. The water didn't bother her. She didn't carry a phone, nor did she have a watch, so there was no fear of damaging electronics.

The rain also helped remind her of the time she'd spent in the surf—more than once. Ice-cold water swelling around her, body covered in sand and debris.

Her damp shoulders pressed against the side of her RV as she watched the figure approaching her.

Waldo Strange the Third was hurrying towards her, hunched, moving fast, and shooting furtive glances over his shoulder.

He was an odd man. A part of Anna distantly wondered if she should have handed him over to the cops at her first chance but she'd gone with her gut on this one. She didn't believe he was involved in her sister's disappearance.

The police radio she kept in the RV had also confirmed this. No other bodies found at the house. Signs of multiple assailants' muddy footprints in the backyard.

There was still the chance that Waldo *was* one of the people who had burned her sister's house, left behind to contaminate or clean up the crime scene, but she didn't believe this either.

Without external resources, she had to go with her instincts. And now, standing in the rain, and watching the burglar hasten towards her, she felt as if she'd made the right call.

Plus, she'd installed a tracking app on his phone without him knowing. If he'd decided to book it, she would've found him... and been far less pleasant about it.

Anna crinkled the bag of jewelry she'd taken off the strange man in one hand.

This had been his incentive to return... plus the slew of threats she'd issued regarding bodily harm if he'd scarpered.

Now, though, he hastened towards her, still shooting glances back. His feet tapped against the wet sidewalk, and in one hand, he clutched a white door camera.

"I got it," he said breathlessly, hastening towards her, and wincing against the rain.

She barely even noticed the water, reaching out to accept the camera.

"Did you get the file drive?" she asked.

"It's a cheapo model," he said. "The SS2. It records directly to an onboard hard-drive."

She nodded, impressed. "You know your security cameras."

"And locks. And safes. And security systems. And alarm response times." He puffed his chest a bit as he rattled this off, grinning at her.

Their eyes met, and she quirked an eyebrow. She had sea-green eyes, a shade darker than his emerald ones. She wondered if this hinted at the darkness she'd witnessed over the years.

One thing could be said for Waldo Strange: unlike Anna, he was a cheerful soul.

Even with two tissues plugging each bleeding nostril, he was grinning as he accepted the bag of jewelry in return for the stolen camera.

"So," he said casually, "Guess I'm off then, huh?"

"Go inside," she said.

"Right. Inside it is. Good suggestion." He stepped past her, sighing as he did.

She followed him back into the RV, pausing in the doorway to glance around, looking down the end of Pine Street. They were parked in an abandoned lot behind an old school. The cops were still on the other end of the roadway.

The sound of the radio chatter could now be heard as she closed the door behind her, entering her mobile home.

By the sound of things, police were still sweeping through the wreckage of the burnt home.

But still no notifications of any more bodies.

Anna was finding that her relief was quickly being replaced by rage.

Someone had burned her baby sister's house to the ground. Was Beth on the run? Was she in hiding? Or had someone taken her?

Anna's eyes narrowed as she clicked her fingers towards Waldo. "Phone."

"What's the magic word?" Waldo said.

"Want to keep your teeth?"

"Exactly," he muttered, handing over his phone. "App is already installed," he said. "Hope you don't mind, but I deleted the new one you added. Didn't really go with the color scheme I was going for."

She glanced at him, and he winked back.

She took his phone and the camera, placing both on the kitchen table. Then, she swiped on the phone until the screen connected to the pilfered security cam.

As she scrolled through the footage, Waldo leaned over her shoulder, pointing out different details. "That's the front door," he said, tapping the screen. "And that's the house. See?"

Anna did. The blue and violet colors of her sister's home were visible in the grainy footage.

She cycled through, staring as midnight turned to morning, and the house remained standing.

She glanced at the timestamp on the bottom of the phone, double-checking it was the correct date.

"See? I'm not there. No hide or tail... that's the expression right? So... mind if I skedaddle?"

"Be quiet," she said simply. "Please," she added, if only to avoid another jibe about words magical or otherwise.

Anna ignored him, focusing on the screen. The footage was grainy, but she could still make out the sudden glow of flames licking at the windows.

She paused the footage.

Two AM.

The fire had started at two in the morning.

"See! See!" He exclaimed. "Long before I was even there."

She fast-forwarded, looking for evidence of Waldo showing up at the scene. At Five AM, she spotted a car rolling down the block. The car disappeared. A few seconds later, a tall, gangly fellow brushed past a first responder. Waldo in a lab coat and blue booties, approached the house, which, three hours after the fire had started, was already smoldering thanks to the ministrations of the fire department.

No evidence of scorch marks or ash. No sign that he'd been in the house earlier.

He was whistling cheerfully as he approached the blaze.

A few seconds later, she spotted as he stumbled out of the house.

She frowned.

He hadn't mentioned this part.

"What's this?" she said.

"Er... Oh... yeah... That..."

She stared as he tripped over the front steps, his face pale, his eyes wide. He stumbled towards a cop and kept jamming a finger over his shoulder, babbling inaudibly in the video.

"You found the bodies?" she said.

Waldo grimaced. "Yeah... yeah, one might say I stumbled on to them."

"Yikes."

"Tell me about it."

Anna returned her attention to the screen. Waldo was hyperventilating in the image, breathing into his hands, and looking on the verge of a panic attack.

"You look scared," she said cheerfully.

"It's all a bluff."

"Oh, yuck. Is that throw-up part also a bluff?"

He muttered something under his breath.

But now, Anna had seen enough. Either Waldo was the best actor she'd ever seen or he was telling the truth. Then again, if he really was ataraxic and the panic and vomit she saw in the footage was faked...

No, she couldn't move forward if she was indecisive. For now, she needed to pick a line to follow. Waldo Strange hadn't expected to find bodies. He had arrived three hours after the blaze. And even if he'd doubled back, to try and throw someone off the scent, why would he have spoken to the cops? Their bodycams would've spotted his face.

No... No, he wasn't involved.

She turned to Waldo, who was still standing over her shoulder. Her voice softening, she said, "You were right. You had nothing to do with this."

GUARDIAN'S VENGEANCE

Waldo shrugged, a lopsided grin on his face. "I told you, I'm a good guy. Just misunderstood."

Anna's eyes darted back to the security footage. She needed to find any clues about who had started the fire and taken her sister. She clicked through the footage, watching as the firefighters battled the blaze and the police began to investigate.

And then she saw something.

It was a figure, darting through the backyard of her sister's house. Anna paused the footage, staring at the screen. She realized a second later she was watching herself chase after Waldo.

She cycled back, towards two AM, before the blaze had started.

She rewound the footage. But no cars appeared on the road. No, figures appeared.

"What time did you see that unmarked car you mentioned?" she said.

"About five-thirty," he said. "After I..."

"Threw up?"

"Endured a bought of indigestion. I think it was the curry rice I had last night."

His cheerful, unrelenting prattle had a strangely soothing effect on her. As if the inanity helped her to focus on one thing at a time.

She found now, having decided Waldo was innocent, that she didn't much mind the career burglar.

So far, he'd proven useful.

She scrolled in the footage, once more, to five thirty, keeping an eye on the road for the aforementioned unmarked vehicle. She briefly wondered how her old teammate, Casper would handle the situation. The friendly Ghost, as he was called, had a way with tech. Sometimes, she even found she missed her old friend.

She focused on the screen again, channeling her inner Casper.

And there it was. The car was parked a block away from the house, and the driver was watching the scene unfold. Anna couldn't make out the driver's face.

She turned to Waldo. "Did you see who was driving that car?"

"Wish I could say I did," he replied. "But I was too busy puking my guts out."

Waldo leaned in closer to the screen, his eyes scanning the footage. Anna watched him for a moment, wondering if she could trust him. He had a criminal record, after all.

Suddenly, Waldo pointed to the screen. "There!" he said. "Did you see that?"

Anna rewound the footage and watched as a dark figure darted across the yard. She couldn't make out who it was, but it was definitely a person. She felt a thrill of excitement.

The person approached the unmarked car and slipped into the backseat.

Only then did the vehicle begin to move, hastening away from the crime scene.

"No license plate," she pointed out.

"What? Shit."

"Back windows are bulletproof. Front driver side isn't."

"Er... how can you tell?"

"Front window is rolled down. Bullet proof glass would be too thick. But the back windows reflect light differently."

She rattled this all off, allowing him a glimpse at her own thought process.

"So... that's definitely a cop car, right?"

"You said the driver carried himself like a cop, huh?"

"Yeah. Definitely. I know cops."

"How many times have you been arrested?"

"I don't remember. But I'm telling you, those guys were cops."

She stared at the screen, frowning. "This town still only has the one precinct?"

He hesitated. "What are you thinking?"

"I'm thinking..." she trailed off, frowning. "Want to make some extra cash?"

He eyed her suspiciously. "If I say no, am I free to go?"

She considered this. Part of her wondered if she ought to call Casper, her old SEAL buddy. He leaved nearby... at least within a couple of states. But no... no, time was of the essence. She glanced at Waldo then nodded once.

"How much cash we talking?"

"An ounce of gold."

"Wait... serious?"

"Mhmm."

He glanced around her RV.

"Don't get any ideas," she said. She could've lied, saying something like it's not here, or I'll have to pick it up from home... But Anna had never been a fan of lying. Not even for utilitarian means. And so she simply said, "Deal or not?"

"An ounce... that's what? Two grand above spot?" He flashed a grin. "Deal. So what do you have in mind? Wh... why are you looking at me like that. Your smile is scaring me."

"I thought you didn't get scared."

"What's the plan, lady?"

"Anna," she said softly. "Call me Anna."

"So what's the plan, Anna?"

"You know cops, right? We need to find that car... so... I need you to create a bit of a disturbance."

She flashed another wicked smile at the uncertain look on his face. Then, she put her RV in gear once more, pulling away from the curb.

Chapter 8

Anna stood in the alley near the chain-link fence, waiting for the sound of mayhem.

She kept shooting glances over her shoulder, down the side street, making sure that none of the officers from the precinct attached to the parking lot were coming for her. As of yet, she'd gone unnoticed.

Anna's eyes flicked from one security camera to another. It had taken her nearly five minutes to plot a course that perfectly made use of the camera's blindspots. Ordinarily, the precinct wouldn't have blind spots, that is, if not for recent construction apparently underway.

Now, where she crouched by the fence, she was shielded in the shadow of an upraised backhoe's digging bucket. The scent of tilled earth and mud lingered on the air.

"Come on," she muttered under her breath, still waiting and listening.

Waldo had exactly one job. Could she trust the guy? No. Of course not. But could she rely on him to do almost anything for an ounce of solid gold? Yes. That she could rely on.

She was here to find the unmarked, bulletproof car. The one that had been spotted outside her sister's place right after the fire had started. And while trespassing in a precinct parking lot wasn't a very smart idea, sometimes one had to crack a few eggs to make an omelet.

Suddenly, there was a loud smashing sound followed by a distant wail. She blinked... had he thrown something through the front window?

Bold.

She heard shouting a second later, the sound of running footsteps from around the front of the building. The facade was currently out of sight.

She waited patiently.

The alarm continued, and she heard more voices as officers hastened from the precinct in pursuit of Waldo Strange.

Once she was sure the commotion had died down, and all eyes would be directed towards whatever mayhem Mr. Strange had decided to cause, she hastened towards the fence, scaling it quickly. It was topped with barbed wire, which was why she had removed her jacket and had it wrapped over one arm.

Reaching the top, she carefully draped the fabric over the sharp barbs, before lowering herself down to the other side. She landed with a thud and quickly straightened up, her eyes scanning for any signs of movement or life.

She was in luck—all seemed clear.

Anna hurried across the lot, weaving between parked cars, checking the makes and models. The entire time she kept glancing over her shoulder, expecting an officer to appear at any moment and demand to know what she was doing there.

But none came.

Her gaze rapidly scanned the parking lot, searching for the unmarked police vehicle. But most of the cars on this side of the building were patrol vehicles. She frowned as she slipped from one car to the next. Where was her target?

Pulling her phone from her pocket, she glanced at the still screenshot of the vehicle in question. It was then that she heard it—the creak of a door being opened.

Anna ducked behind the nearest vehicle, peering out from between two tires. Her heart raced as she watched two officers emerge from the back exit, their faces illuminated in the moonlight.

They were coming her way.

"Threw a damn trashcan through the front window," one of them was saying. "They see the guy?"

"We'll find him," said the other. The two of them were moving swiftly and were almost in line with her hiding spot.

She waited quietly, keeping low, listening intently. As the cops veered past her, they slipped into one of the parked vehicles, gunned the engine, and sped away. She frowned after the glare of their taillights.

Anna slowly straightened, peering along the side of the building. No sign of the unmarked vehicle here... Maybe it was out on the job?

Maybe it wasn't a cop car after all...

She felt her frustration mounting but she inhaled slowly, steadying her nerves and compartmentalizing her emotions.

The third car. She just had to make it to the third car parked against the precinct. Then she could reassess. Nothing mattered but reaching that car.

The familiar mantra of setting short-form goals propelled her forward. She hastened towards the waiting vehicle.

And then she paused.

She was nearly at the edge of the building. She could hear a loud commotion coming from the front as officers milled around the scene of the busted window.

Breathing softly, she peered around the edge of the building, careful not to move too swiftly.

The front steps were filled with activity.

Officers were milling around the broken glass, examining it and talking to each other in stern voices. Pairings were heading out in different directions, presumably to search for the vandal who had caused the damage.

The atmosphere was tense, and she could feel the anger radiating from the officers as they searched for any clues that would help them track down the criminal responsible.

Anna breathed a sigh of relief—they hadn't noticed her yet.

That's when she saw it.

The unmarked car.

It was parked in the far corner of the lot, almost obscured by the shadow of the precinct wall. Anna's heart leapt with excitement. She had found it. The only problem? It was on the opposite side of the milling officers. She'd have to slip past them to reach it. But how? There was no way she could go unnoticed.

She hesitated, then decided the best way forward was a quick trip back. She turned, hastening in the direction she'd come, racing towards the mesh fence and barbed wire barricade once more.

As she dropped to the other side of the fence once more, Anna heard the sound of footsteps. She spun around, her heart racing.

It was Waldo, panting and gasping for breath.

"I... I lost them," he wheezed. "I don't think they saw me. But we gotta get outta here now!"

"Why'd you double back?"

"You still owe me. Two ounces of gold."

"One ounce," she snapped. "I'm good for it."

"Well... don't mind me if I don't just take your word for it."

"Did you really throw a trash can through the front window of the precinct?"

"I'll never tell."

She rolled her eyes, already moving towards the fence. "I found the car," she replied, gesturing towards the far corner of the lot. "It's on the other side of them."

Waldo's eyes widened as he saw the officers milling around in the distance. "They'll see us for sure," he muttered.

Anna took a deep breath. "We just have to be quick. Follow me."

She led the way, to the opposite side of the street, waiting for two cops to hurry past, where they hastened towards an empty business complex. Keeping low, Anna darted from car to car. Waldo followed close behind, his eyes darting nervously from side to side.

As they neared the unmarked vehicle, Anna could feel her heart pounding in her chest. She caught the glint of a license plate, which made her pause. There hadn't been a plate in the footage earlier, but it was the same car. She was certain.

She glanced over at Waldo, who was trying to catch his breath. Together, they approached the vehicle.

Anna's hand was steady as she reached out to try the door handle. It was locked. She cursed under her breath. "I need your keys," she said.

"What?"

"Your keys," she whispered. "The ones that are making that ungodly racket every time you move."

Reluctantly he produced the keys, handing them to her. She slipped the items off the ring one by one and handed them back in a loose handful.

"Well, that was a fun ritual," Waldo muttered, trying not to drop any of the keys as he moved them into his pocket.

She ignored him, stretching out the ring of metal to form a pick. It was an old car—too old to have modern safety measures. Her nimble fingers worked quickly as she jimmied the lock, and it took only a few seconds before she heard the click of the lock giving way.

Anna grinned in triumph as she opened the door and slipped inside.

The car was empty, but she could see that it had been recently used. There were papers scattered on the passenger seat, and a faint smell of cigarette smoke lingered in the air. Anna quickly scanned the papers, looking for any clues as to who had been driving the car. But the items were blank traffic tickets. She ignored these, moving swiftly. She needed a name.

She opened the glove compartment, but it was empty, save for a service revolver.

She focused on her breathing, containing frustration, ignoring the fear of discovery. The mission was all that mattered: she needed to find out whose car this was.

Then, her eyes landed on the radio receiver attached to the front of the vehicle. She leaned forward, examining the device.

"Find anything?" Waldo whispered.

"No."

"We really should get going," he muttered.

"Anyone coming this way?"

"Yeah. Two guys."

She turned sharply and realized he was right. A couple of officers were strolling in their direction.

"Why didn't you say something sooner?" she hissed.

"I'm saying something now!"

The two officers didn't look as if they were approaching *this* car, but they would spot the intruders within a few moments.

Anna wasn't willing to stop yet, though. She needed to find something. Anything.

Desperately, she searched under the seats. Pulling at the carpets. Still nothing.

"They're getting closer," Waldo hissed.

She ignored him still, pulling on the sun visor over the window.

A set of keys fell out, jangling as they struck the back of her hand. And there, tucked under a strap on the visor, she spotted a single photo. She stared. It was a photo of two children: both of them staring out with smiling faces.

The children's smiles haunted her, forcing her mind back to her nephew and niece.

She forced the emotions away, shelving the swirling grief and fear on behalf of her sister's family. She couldn't live in it. Not now. She would become useless if she let emotions cripple her. Like a shark, she had to keep moving.

She let out a faint, shaking breath and took the photo.

"We have to leave, now!" Waldo was saying, tugging at her arm. But then he cursed.

The cops' voices were rising.

"Hey!" they were saying. "Hey, you!"

"Shit," Waldo whispered. "Too late."

Anna tucked the pilfered photo in her pocket. She then reached out, snagging Waldo by the arm and yanking him into the car. He spilled over her lap, and she shoved him. "Get in!" she commanded.

He moved with surprising agility, scrambling over her and sliding into the passenger seat. He was staring at her, wide-eyed and horrified. "What the hell are you doing?"

She jammed the keys that had fallen from the sun visor into the ignition.

"Hey!" the cops were shouting. "Hey, stop!"

Anna revved the engine, her heart racing. She put the car in drive and slammed her foot on the gas. The tires squealed as she peeled out of the parking lot.

Waldo was cursing beside her, his hands gripping the dashboard.

GUARDIAN'S VENGEANCE

"Stop freaking out," she snapped.

Anna glanced in the rearview mirror. Sure enough, the two officers were standing in the middle of the parking lot, staring after them. But they weren't giving chase as if they were too stunned to react. Then, they both turned racing towards their own vehicle. One of the men was speaking hastily into a radio receiver.

She could hear his announcement over the radio in the stolen car.

"In pursuit of stolen vehicle, license plate number 6K77V2. Two suspects, a man and a woman. Caucasian, early thirties. Suspected to be armed and dangerous."

Anna's grip tightened on the steering wheel.

Waldo was staring at her with a mixture of fear and admiration. "That was crazy," he said. "You're crazy. Who the hell are you?"

Anna bit her lip, her mind racing. She needed to find a place to hide, somewhere the cops wouldn't think to look for them.

She let out a breath she didn't realize she'd been holding.

Waldo didn't say anything, which was a first. He was still staring at her, his eyes wide with disbelief.

She knew what he was thinking. He probably thought she was crazy. Maybe she was.

But she had a job to do. And she wasn't going to let anyone get in her way.

She drove in silence for several moments at a breakneck pace, the only sound the hum of the engine and the rush of wind through the open windows.

Finally, Waldo spoke. "So... what now?"

Anna didn't answer at first. She was still reeling from the adrenaline rush of the past few minutes and checking the mirrors to make sure they had enough of a head start that the cops weren't in pursuit.

Then she remembered the photo in her pocket. "Now," she muttered, swerving sharply into a grocery store parking lot. Sirens wailed behind them, but for the moment, the cops were still giving chase. "We ditch the car."

She flung open the door, snatched the keys, and tossed them into the back seat. Waldo hastened after her.

"W-what? Wasn't the whole point *to find* the car?"

"No. The point was to find out whoever was in it, whoever was staking out the house before it burned down with two men inside." She was marching towards the storefront now. "We need a change of clothing so they can't recognize us," she muttered. "Maybe some hair dye. And you need a bath."

"Ouch. Hurtful."

She kept tapping her hand against her pocket, feeling the crinkle of the photograph she'd found in the car. Two children... How hard would it be to find the officer whose children these were?

Not hard at all.

Not with the advent of social media.

She'd go through the online, public-facing website with police photos. Then compare them to social media profiles paired with the two children. It would take some time, but it would provide a likely outcome.

She stepped through the sliding doors of the grocery store without missing a beat, turning her face to avoid the cameras above on instinct alone. She spotted multiple points of exit, and the two security guards chumming it up by an in-store pizza restaurant.

Her hand grazed the photograph in her pocket, and her mind shifted once again to her sister's family. Fear threatened to flood her, and again, she doubled her pace, moving fast toward a rack of women's clothes.

Get changed. Dye her hair. Slip out the back.

Then find the cops who'd been sneaking around her sister's burnt home.

Chapter 9

Anna sat in her RV, peering at the house at the end of the block, through the encircling black fence.

She was relieved to be alone again.

Waldo Strange had taken his payment and vanished once they'd left the grocery store.

Now, sitting in her RV, in the tranquil silence of the familiar mobile home, she glanced at the cheap smartphone on the chair next to her. Another purchase along with the hair dye which she hadn't ended up using.

The screen on the phone displayed a picture of a stoic police officer glaring stone-faced at the camera.

The man in the picture was tall and broad-shouldered, with a sharp jawline and dark eyes that seemed to pierce right through you. His skin had an olive sheen, and his left cheek was marred by a long, jagged scar that curved down from just below his eye to the corner of his mouth.

"A bit on the nose, isn't it?" she muttered to herself, frowning at the face in front of her.

His eyes were staring at her, communicating a glower, even via screen. She frowned back, drumming her fingers against the steering wheel. The second knuckle on her pointer had a shrapnel scar across the digit that made it difficult to bend the finger completely.

Her body was covered in such scars—mementos of a kind.

She studied the picture of the man. She'd found him on social media, matching his police photograph with an online profile. She'd found the two kids in the photos, matching them to the image she'd found in the unmarked car they'd abandoned in the shopping center's parking lot.

This was the owner of that car. The same car that had idled outside her sister's burning home without attempting to offer any aid. The same car that had been a vehicle for a hooded figure fleeing her sister's residence. She scowled even more deeply, tapping her fingers against the steering wheel.

"How do you afford a place like that on a police salary?" she muttered, staring through the windshield at the enormous home behind the wrought-iron fence.

She'd been watching Officer Malcolm Davis' home for the better part of a half hour. She didn't want to go in half-cocked; reconnaissance was key to any successful operation.

She reached for the small notepad and pen lying on the passenger seat, jotting down a few notes. Two security cameras, East wing.

No lookouts. An electric gate. Fence ten feet tall.

She cataloged all this information, brow furrowed as she made notes of it in her small, leather notebook.

The notebook helped her think. Writing down the information helped her remember it.

She committed the information to memory and then slipped out of the car.

"Let's see what you know..."

She began to move towards the house, cautiously, under the cover of the fallen night. The moon had even done her a favor by hiding behind the clouds, and only allowing the occasional beam of light to stray through the cottony canopy.

She was careful not to get too close to the nearest camera's field of vision. It was something of a strain on her mind to constantly catalog the ways something like this could go wrong.

She took a deep breath and began to climb the fence, using the metal bars as footholds until she was at the top. Her fingers gripped tightly onto one of the spikes as she pulled herself over and dropped down into Malcolm Davis's yard.

She landed lightly on her feet and crouched low, listening for any sound that might indicate a presence within the house. The wind rustled through leaves and branches above her head, but otherwise, it was silent.

Satisfied that she wasn't detected, she moved silently towards one of the windows on the east wing of Malcolm Davis' home.

And that's when the front door swung open.

Four men emerged, smoking and talking amongst themselves.

She stiffened, staring at the door, remaining in the shadows, and pressing her back against the wall where she could feel the faint outline of the stone.

Her eyes fixated on the men, studying them closely. All were dressed in dark clothing, and she could just make out the outlines of handguns tucked away in their waistbands.

"What do you think about the job?" one of them asked.

"It's risky," replied another. "But it should pay off if we do it right."

The other two nodded in agreement, but none elaborated on what exactly this 'job' entailed. The four men continued to talk as they stepped onto the patio, not noticing her presence at all.

She watched them from her hiding spot near one of the windows, straining to pick up any details that might help her get closer to understanding what they were discussing.

Were they involved in the disappearance of her sister? The burning of their home?

She still didn't even know if her sister's family was still alive. This thought sent a jolt of anger through her, but her eyes remained fixated on the porch.

Suddenly, her attention was drawn to one of the men, who seemed to be looking in her direction. She held her breath, her heart racing as she watched him approach the railing to the porch, his hand moving towards his gun.

But just as he was about to pull out the weapon, his phone rang.

He answered it, and Anna could hear a muffled voice on the other end of the line.

"Sorry guys, I have to take this," he said, stepping away from the others.

Anna seized the opportunity to move closer to the group, staying low and silent as she crept toward them. She couldn't make out the conversation on the phone, but the man's body language was tense and agitated.

"Is everything okay?" one of the others asked, eyeing him warily.

"No, it's not," the man replied, his voice low and urgent. "We've got a problem."

Anna's heart raced as she listened, trying to piece together what was happening.

Suddenly, the man on the phone hung up and turned back towards the group.

"We have to leave," he said, his voice urgent. "Now."

The others looked at him in confusion but didn't argue as they quickly made their way back towards the house.

Anna watched as they disappeared inside, her mind racing with questions.

Who were these men, and what was their connection to Malcolm Davis?

And what was this "job" they were discussing?

She hesitated only briefly... There was no time to skulk about in the dark. Not now.

She needed to enter the house. She scanned along the building, searching for an accessible window. There, on the second floor. One of the windows was open.

She hesitated, listening intently.

What was she hoping to hear? The sound of her sister's voice? Her nephew or niece calling out? Her brother-in-law pleading for mercy?

She hesitated.

Her mind shifted to her brother-in-law once more. Tom Gabriel had taken Beth's last name. He was a meek, mild-mannered sort. An accountant. He was also waspishly smart, and an excellent father from what she'd heard via email.

Was he the source of this trouble?

Who'd brought the danger to Beth's doorstep?

She frowned.

Please help.

The text message still haunted her. She shivered briefly, shaking her head in frustration.

Then, she turned, moving towards the window. She stood under it, about fifteen feet away. The sound of the voices had faded now, and she stood in the shadow of the red brick wall, peering up at the window, head tilted.

She listened to the breeze.

No one called out.

No one had spotted her.

They rarely did.

She then took a running start and flung herself up the faux brick facade.

Her fingers gripped tightly onto the uneven bricks as she climbed, her muscles straining with the effort. She hoisted herself up, one hand at a time, until she reached the window.

She peered inside, her eyes scanning the room for any sign of danger. The room was dark, but she could make out the outlines of furniture and a bed against the far wall.

Taking a deep breath, she swung her legs over the windowsill and slipped inside the room.

She landed softly on the carpeted floor, her eyes quickly adjusting to the darkness. She could see a door on the opposite wall, leading out into the hallway. She moved towards it silently, her heart pounding in her chest as she listened for any sound from the other side.

She turned the handle and pushed the door open, peeking out into the hallway.

The hallway was empty, but she could hear the sound of voices coming from somewhere further down.

As she got closer, she could make out the same four men standing in a room at the end of the hallway. They were facing away from her, their attention focused on something in the center of the room.

Anna moved closer, frowning.

The four men were staring at something on the ground.

She frowned, following their gazes.

For a moment, in horror, she half expected to find a corpse lying in full view.

Except it wasn't a corpse. Not yet.

Not quite yet.

But she'd found Malcolm Davis.

The cop whose car had been outside her sister's place was lying on the ground, moaning. His face was covered in cuts and bruises. His hands were bleeding, and his pants were stained as well.

The man was nearly unrecognizable due to the beating he'd clearly endured.

A new man, who hadn't been on the smoke break, stood in this room, scowling down at Mr. Davis. This man was dark-skinned with a pronounced underbite and a mean expression. His fists were rubbed raw, suggesting that his tender mercies were scrawled across Mr. Davis' face.

Anna's mind raced as she tried to piece together what she was seeing. Why would these men beat up a cop? And what was their connection to her sister's disappearance?

She waited, hidden in the shadows, as the men continued their conversation. They were speaking in low tones, making it difficult for Anna to make out what they were saying but she was determined to get closer.

Slowly, she moved towards the room, inching her way forward until she was just a few feet away from the door. She could hear the men more clearly now, and she strained to listen in on their conversation.

"We have to get rid of him," one of the men said, his voice low and urgent. "He knows too much. We can't afford to let him live."

"He might still be useful," snapped the thug with the underbite and bruised knuckles. "He's a tough son of a bitch."

Malcolm Davis wasn't moving, his eyes sealed shut, his hands tied behind his back.

Who would do this to a cop?

Finally, though, the thug with the underbite sighed. "Fine... fine... The boss says so?"

"Yeah," snapped another. "He says so. So why not just get it over with, huh?"

Malcolm was shaking his head, whimpering as he lay there in a pool of his own blood. Underbite raised his weapon, shrugging with indifference. It was as if he'd been asked to take out the trash, and now had resigned himself to the mundane task.

A sharp *clack* announced a fresh round being chambered.

Anna had to make a split-second decision.

She didn't know this man. And for all she knew, he'd been involved in her sister's disappearance... or worse.

But if that was true, then he also might have information. Anyone in the room might've. She couldn't let them put a bullet in his brain.

But she also wasn't stupid. A closed room full of armed gunmen? The chances of catching a bullet were too high. She wasn't a superhero. Without proper planning and preparation, much of her advantage was undermined by being outnumbered in a tight space.

She assessed the situation quickly, eyes landing on the man who'd issued the order. He was likely in charge.

Good enough.

She lunged into the room before a gun could be fired, snaking her arm around the thug's neck as quick as a slipknot. His sharp cry was cut off by her forearm against his windpipe. She squeezed tightly, yanking him back to the doorway as the other gunmen shouted in surprise.

Underbite was pointing his weapon at her now but hesitated due to her human shield.

"Drop it!" she warned, her voice calm, "Or I'll snap his neck."

The man she was choking gurgled, trying to yank free, but it was no use.

The other men looked around in shock, unsure of how to handle the situation.

"Drop it, now!" Anna said again, her voice steel.

Had she made a mistake?

It was all a matter of instinct and probability. This was why a girl needed a plan. But there simply hadn't been time.

"Do it!" choked out the man she held. "Do it, now!"

Finally, Underbite lowered his weapon slowly, the barrel aimed at the floor.

The other gunmen were all tense, staring at her. She glanced over her shoulder, scanning the wall.

Then, she said, "Who do you guys work for?"

None of them answered. They just stared at her, hesitant.

She felt the man under her arm tense.

"Boss would want this dealt with. Either way," Underbite was saying, his voice rising in volume.

She could see him psyching himself up from a mile away.

The others were also waiting for his response. She glanced down at Malcolm Davis. He was still lying on his stomach, his hands behind his back. She spotted his belt, full of police items, including keys, a gun, and pepper spray lying on the floor by a stain of his own blood.

But she only had an eye for the utility knife.

She'd have to move fast.

Underbite began to raise his gun, so she acted.

She shoved the thug toward him and lashed out with her heel, connecting with the light switch she'd spotted when looking at the wall.

The late hour and dark night aided in the chaos. Bullets exploded in the pitch-black room as she flung herself to the ground. For now, she was the target, but she was no longer standing in the door.

She snatched at the flashlight from the policeman's belt where she'd spotted it lying seconds before. She turned it on and flung the extremely bright beam into one corner.

One moment, dark, the next, a burst of high-power light, blinding them--the thugs yelled, shooting at the light.

Chaos reigned, if only for a moment. As she crouched by Davis, she hissed, "Run."

She had the utility knife in one hand and sawed through his ropes.

The man was still groaning, still only semi-conscious.

She finally pulled the gun from the belt.

"She's there! On the floor!" someone shouted.

But she stopped him cold, two shots to the chest.

He grunted, tumbling back. She fired once more at a man whose dark form was barely visible. The muzzle flash had alerted her to the location of the men, and she'd committed to memory. As she shoved Malcolm through the door, she felt something hot graze past her arm and cheek. but she reached the hall, shoving Malcolm again, sending him ahead of her.

"Run!" she yelled.

Chapter 10

Anna pushed Malcolm ahead of her, and he gasped in pain from his injuries as he stumbled forward down the hall.

She fired twice more, gunshots echoing through the mansion as she laid covering fire. Bullets struck the wooden frame of the darkened room where the gunmen were milling.

They cursed, ducking back inside as wood chips exploded from the frame, splinters falling around them.

"Move!" she commanded.

The injured police officer was gasping heavily, clutching at his right arm, which dangled limply at his side. His face was a mess of cuts and bruises, yet she could still see his look of panic. His eyes flared, and his breath came in quick puffs. He stumbled and nearly fell, but she caught his arm, pushing him forward.

The gunmen behind them returned fire now. She cursed, shoving Malcolm into a side room as bullets whizzed past them.

He hit the ground, gasping.

"Get up!" she commanded. She snatched his arm, tugging him to his feet, her own muscles straining.

She shot twice more through the doorway, without aiming, simply to warn them off.

She was running low on ammo.

The gunmen were still shouting, and she could now hear their footsteps pounding down the hall. Her eyes darted to the large window in the wall, facing the black iron gate encircling the moonlit property.

"Wh-who are you?" Malcolm's voice trembled, but she didn't respond.

She still didn't know if he was directly involved in her sister's disappearance. Technically, she hadn't seen him on the footage outside Beth's house, only his car.

But undercover cops didn't usually live in mansions either.

She pushed him forward, and said, "Going through the window. Brace yourself."

She tugged at the windowsill, her fingers scrambling desperately for a solid purchase.

Malcolm stumbled forward, flinching as the gunmen's bullets pinged off the wall.

The window slid open, and she heaved him through, the cold night air rushing inwards.

They tumbled out into the garden, the moonlight barely illuminating the grass. She hit the ground, fifteen feet below, tucking her body, and striking the damp earth shoulder first.

The grass and mud cushioned the fall somewhat, but she still felt it jolt through her body, and she gasped as air left her lungs. Malcolm was struggling to rise again, his injured arm providing no support for his equally battered body.

She desperately tugged at his arm. Now, she could hear the gunmen reaching the room behind them, their shouts echoing out into the night.

"Get up!" she commanded, dragging at Malcolm's limp arm.

He groaned but complied, his legs shaking beneath him.

She pulled him across the grass, struggling to keep her footing as they hurried towards the gate. The ground sloped downwards, and they were soon running, her boots pounding against the ground.

The gate was close now, and she could feel the gunmen's bullets whizzing past her, striking the iron. The gunshots echoed into the night.

She pushed Malcolm aside and scrambled up the gate, her hands slipping on the iron bars. She flung her jacket over the barbed wire once more but missed a section in her haste. A hot flash of pain lanced through her leg as razor-sharp metal gouged her.

She cursed but extended a hand back towards Malcolm. "Come on. Now or never!"

He struggled, reaching up towards her, his eyes wide and desperate. His hand was slick with blood from his injuries. His other hand didn't move, still hanging limply at his side. She snatched at his arm and bracing herself against the gate, she tried to pull with all her might.

The barbs dug even deeper into her thigh, but she ignored the pain, ignored the wet blood now spilling down her leg. Malcolm's feet scrambled on the ridge between the metal bars, and he found a foothold, releasing some of the tension in Anna's arms.

She yanked with all her might, and he gasped as he was tugged on top of the fence. She allowed herself to fall now, dragging him with her jacket as if he were on a sled over the barbed wire.

He landed next to her. More bullets struck the ground.

She spotted the gunmen now climbing through the window facing the lawn.

"Go!" she yelled, pushing Malcolm forward.

The two of them ran, the night air rushing around them.

The gunmen were still shouting and their footsteps were getting closer.

They sprinted down the street, their breaths coming rapidly. Anna's eyes moved towards her RV, where she'd parked it, hidden under the shadow of a copse of trees. The gate was still closed behind them, and she heard loud cursing as the gunmen realized they would either have to scale the fence, or rush to the entry point, five hundred or so yards away. Again, even now, Anna kept the cameras in mind, which she'd cataloged in her small journal.

"Who-who are you?" Malcolm kept repeating. His voice was shaking horribly, and his face looked even worse when caught by the moonlight, revealing the wounds and fresh cuts. She spotted the old scar she'd seen in his photograph, meandering down his cheek.

There would be more scars after tonight.

If he survived.

"Move!" she repeated.

She heard the grumble of an engine behind her, suggesting that some of the gunmen had reached a vehicle. She spotted the metal gate slowly opening on automatic hinges.

She sprinted towards her RV, still pushing Malcolm ahead of her.

He stumbled, and she grabbed the back of his jacket, tugging him forward.

The gunmen were now gaining ground, and she spotted them in a black Jeep, tearing through the now-open gate. The engine roared as they chased them down.

She reached the RV, and reached for the handle on the door, yanking it open.

She shoved Malcolm inside, and then jumped in after him, slamming the door shut. She'd covered her license plate in mud earlier, and now, she was grateful for the precaution.

The engine turned over on the third try, and the RV lurched forward, bumping over the grass as they sped away.

"We're never going to outrun them in this," Malcolm said, his voice full of horror.

"This?" she said, tongue tucked in her cheek as she navigated back onto the road and swerved around a switchback. "This RV has some upgrades, bud. Sit down and buckle up."

She'd had work done on her vehicle. The engine had been replaced by a military-grade one repurposed from a decommissioned tank, and the suspension and brakes had been reinforced.

She glanced in the rearview mirror, watching as the Jeep swerved onto the same road, taking the switchback a bit too fast, and veering off onto the detritus surrounding the road, before returning back to the asphalt.

The two vehicles tore down the tree-lined path, speeding under the watchful moon. Her RV was quicker than most, but the Jeep was also fast.

She felt a thrill of excitement course through her veins as she pushed the engine, her hands gripping the wheel tightly.

The Jeep was still behind them, but it was no longer gaining on them.

She glanced at Malcolm, his face pale and his hand gripping the seat back. In the dim light of the interior RV, his wounds looked even worse.

Did he need a hospital?

Anna cursed. One problem at a time.

The two vehicles raced through the night. The Jeep was slowly falling back as she picked up speed, the old, repurposed engine propelling the vehicle through the night.

She could no longer hear the sound of gunshots, nor could she see the flash of a muzzle.

She swerved down a side road, hoping to cut line of sight. Twice more, she took sharp turns, her vehicle obscured by the trees lining the road. The scenic vista of the Sierra Mountains in the distance cast long shadows over their attempt at an escape.

"Come on, come on," she whispered as she veered down another side road. And then, up ahead, she spotted a small farm.

A barn.

"Quick," she said. "When I tell you, get out and open that door. Okay? Hey, Malcolm. Are you listening?"

"W-what?"

"Now!" she swerved up the dusty driveway. The lights were off in the farmhouse, and she hoped she wouldn't catch a bullet from a trigger-happy denizen.

They skidded on the dusty asphalt, and she came to a halt.

She shot a quick glance over her shoulder.

It was a risky move but they'd outpaced the Jeep for now, and they were no longer in sight, though she could hear the Jeep still rapidly approaching.

"Open the door!" she commanded. "Go, go!"

But Malcolm's head was lolling, his eyes fluttering as he came in and out of consciousness.

She'd have to do it herself.

She jumped out of the vehicle, allowing it to idle forward. She sprinted towards the barn door and grabbed at the wooden plank securing the frame.

She lifted it, even as the RV came towards her. It drifted slowly, but not so lazily that she didn't have to time this perfectly. She pulled the door open, and the RV rolled in, just before the Jeep came into view.

She flung herself inside, slammed the door shut, and leaned against it. The RV bumped against a tractor-mower, groaning and coming to a stop.

The sound of the Jeep's engine came closer, and she stood in the darkness of the barn, breathing heavily. She waited, tense, standing in the dark, inhaling dust and the scent of old straw.

The lights from the farmhouse were still off—she could see the dark structure through gaps in the barn beams.

The sound of the Jeep's engine grew louder, she tensed, but then it began to fade again, suggesting the vehicle was hastening up the long, dusty farm road, away from their temporary hiding spot.

She shot a quick look through the windshield of her RV.

Malcolm was unconscious again.

He'd lost a lot of blood.

Anna took a step back towards her RV but hissed sharply at the pain flaring through her thigh. Her own cut was now aching, and she glanced down to see where fabric and skin alike had ripped.

She shook her head, ignoring the pain. She could tell at a glance it wasn't life-threatening—not like Malcolm's.

A hospital. She needed to get him medical care. Was he even breathing?

Shit. She flung herself into her vehicle once more.

Chapter 11

Anna stood in the doorway of the hospital room after hours. It was nearly midnight, and she'd signed in as Malcolm Davis's concerned wife.

Again, social camouflage was just as useful as warpaint. She'd played the terrified spouse well enough to convince a doctor and two nurses that she could be trusted alone in the room with the injured man.

And now, judging by the increasing beeping sound coming from the heart monitor, Malcolm was coming to.

She glanced over her shoulder through the glass door toward a nurse sitting behind a desk down the hall, yawning and watching re-runs of some soap opera behind the counter looking inattentive at best. Anna reached back and tugged at the privacy curtain to conceal the window, and then she approached the bed.

The scent of antiseptic lingered on the air, and the beeping of the heart monitor grew louder as she drew closer. Anna stopped at the bedside, her eyes fixed on the man in the bed. He was an angry-looking fellow, even with the bruises and bandages. His breathing had grown more steady, and his eyes flickered open as she watched him.

"Who are you?" he asked, his voice hoarse and rough.

Anna forced a smile. "I'm your wife. You don't remember?"

"Funny. Who are you really?"

She shot a look towards the door, her ear cocking for the sounds of anyone walking the halls nearby. Satisfied, she turned back to the bed. "Let's not worry about who I am," Anna said quietly. "Let's worry about you, Mr. Davis."

He tried to sit up in his bed but grimaced and lowered himself again, his blanket bunching around his elbows.

"Wh-what do you want from me?"

"I just saved your life," she replied. "By my count, that puts you in my debt."

He closed his eyes briefly, releasing a long, pent-up breath. He winced again and shifted, his arm—now in a cast—resting on his chest.

"Why were you outside Beth Gabriel's home early this morning?" she said.

He blinked, staring at her.

Clearly, whatever he'd been expecting, it hadn't been this.

"I... I wasn't," he said.

"Your car was."

"I wasn't in it."

"I don't believe you."

He grimaced. "I'm telling the truth. I mean... look at me."

"You're some sort of victim, huh? That's why you own a million-dollar home on a cop salary?"

He shifted uncomfortably. She leaned forward now, crowding his personal space, intentionally trying to discomfort him. "Tell me why you were there?"

She still didn't know that he had been, but she often found the best path to a confession was a direct, insistent line of questioning. He was tired, hurt and scared. Hardly in a great position to keep his wits about him.

She studied him, her face cold and features firm. In times like this, her personable facial symmetry worked against her. The upturned nose, and the church-going girl next door look didn't exactly imbue her words with intimidation.

But the anger in her green eyes, and the tattoos on her forearm hinted at the truth to anyone who'd pay attention.

"I wasn't!" he insisted.

"Then how do you know you weren't in the car? You didn't ask what time. You didn't ask who's Beth Gabriel. You just denied it."

He went quiet. "I..." He loosed a slow breath. "I want a lawyer."

"I'm not a cop," she snorted. "And if you were involved in Beth's death, I'll put two bullets in your spine. So start talking."

"I wasn't in that car," he snapped.

"Who was?"

"My partner."

"Liar," she retorted. "Your partner is in Florida with his wife; I already checked."

He fell quiet.

And now, she was getting a better picture of the man. He was lying, which meant he was scared, which also meant he was likely lying about other things too.

She glared at him, and leaned forward now, pressing her hand hard against his injured arm.

He let out a faint mewl of pain. His heartbeat monitor quickened.

"I don't know..."

But she could see him cracking. Could see the fear in his eyes.

She pulled a knife from her belt, pressing it against his neck now. Her eyes blazed as anger came over her. She was good at controlling her emotions. Good at suppressing and compartmentalizing what she wanted in order to accomplish the mission.

But sometimes, when the dam broke, the water that had long been suppressed came rushing out.

And now, all the suppressed grief, rage, fear, and anger was coming to a point. The knife pressed harder against his throat. "You don't know me," she said quietly, her voice simmering. "But Beth is important to me. I've killed more men than you've likely befriended in your life. I've had to do hard things, but when I have a mission, I make sure it's done. Or I don't come home. Is that clear? Don't make me end you. Where's my sister?"

He stared at her, horrified. And then he stammered, "I didn't know."

"Didn't know what."

His Adam's apple bobbed past the blade. "Didn't know they were going to hurt her," he whispered. "I was just the driver."

"Bullshit."

"I was! I swear!"

"You were in the car!"

"Driving. That's all. I didn't... didn't know about the cargo van."

"What cargo van?"

"Just... What?"

"What cargo van?" she demanded, angling the knife against his throat with a chaffing, razor-burn scrape.

He was starting to panic now. She could see his eyes darting towards the curtained window. His breathing became shallow and ragged; sweat pooled on his forehead; his hands began to shake.

Anna lowered her chin, her eyes boring into him threateningly as she slowly increased the blade's pressure.

Suddenly Malcolm called out. "Nurse! Help!" he screamed in terror as he pushed back against the bed with all his might, trying to escape her grasp.

Anna clapped a hand over his mouth, but too late. The floor squeaked with the rush of the nurse's shoes as she hurried from her soap opera to the room, no doubt expecting some medical emergency. Anna shot to her feet and flew to the door, the nurse stopping short as they reached the room's only entrance at the same moment.

She spotted Anna's glare—spotted the knife—and the nurse's eyes widened. "Security! We need security!"

Anna gave the woman a swift, open-handed shove to the sternum, sending her reeling for the split second she needed.

But Anna's resolve wasn't wavering and she wasn't running. She slammed the door closed, grabbing the resilient, metal-framed guest chair and lodging it under the handle to keep it in place.

The nurse pounded on the door's narrow glass window, but Anna turned away, ignoring her and marching back to the bedside. Her bedside manner was lacking, and her anger was palpable.

"I'm done playing games," she said coldly as she pressed the blade even closer against his neck. "Tell me what happened or I'll start cutting."

He glanced towards the door where the nurse was still banging on the glass. he swallowed, then stammered, "Look... I've been getting a bit of extra. Cop salary doesn't pay, okay? I have medical bills. I was undercover and got shot... I needed some extra cash, but the bosses didn't dole out."

"I get it. You deserved that money... So who was paying you?"

"It's a local outfit. That's all I know. I didn't ask much. They didn't either, just needed me to look the other way on a couple of arrests. That's all."

"And then what?" she demanded. "How is Beth Gabriel involved?"

"I... I didn't know her name. Didn't know who it was until... you know... after."

"After what? Did you burn down the house?"

"No! Look," he said carefully. "I was just..."

The pounding on the door grew louder, and Anna noticed two security guards had shown up. They were making threatening gestures at her. Both of them were trying to force the door open. But the metal chair held firm.

Anna's heart raced, her muscles tense as her mind simulated a dozen different ways this situation could end, several of them involving fresh blood on her knife. But she kept her focus; her eyes remained locked on Malcolm Davis.

"I didn't know," Malcolm's voice was hoarse, barely above a whisper. "I swear, I didn't know about the fire."

Anna's expression remained impassive. "Who did you drive there?"

He swallowed hard, wincing from the pain. "I was contacted by this guy. He didn't give me much, just asked me to drive him somewhere that night."

"And you just agreed?" Anna's tone was skeptical.

"I needed the money," he admitted, shame flickering in his eyes. "He was gone for a while, then came back, all nonchalant. I didn't think much of it."

Anna leaned in closer. "And Beth's house?"

Malcolm's gaze dropped. "That's where I drove him. I didn't know what he was planning. I only heard about the fire later."

Anna straightened up, her mind racing. "Who was this guy who contacted you?"

"It's like I said. Organized crime. They're a newer group in the area."

"What are they called?"

"Los Hermanos," he said.

"Those guys roughing you up at the house didn't look Hispanic," she retorted.

"They've got a mixture, but the bosses? They're old country. I swear it."

"And why were they at my sister's house?"

"I don't know." He shook his head adamantly. "If I did, I would tell you." He winced as she withdrew the knife.

The door was now slowly inching open as the security guards tried to shove in. Both of them had guns, and they were calling out at her. She ignored them.

She fixated her gaze on Malcolm, trying to read him.

His tapestry of cuts made it difficult to detect deception in his features.

She wasn't sure if she was being duped, but she also knew what she'd seen back at that mansion.

"So why were they roughing you up?" she demanded.

"No witnesses," he retorted.

"So you were just a loose end."

"Yeah."

"A loose end for what?" she could feel her frustration growing larger. "These Los Hermanos, where do they meet? Where's their HQ."

"It's an old biker bar just outside Mammoth Lakes," he said. "If I knew anything else, I'd tell you. I swear. You think I want those guys walking around? I'm going to have to skip town as it is."

Suddenly the door to the hospital room slammed open, the metal chair bracing it shooting into the wall as it was knocked loose. The two security guards hastened in, guns raised. "Get on the ground!" they were shouting. "Get down, now!"

Anna was already moving, though. She sprinted for the window, keeping her back in line with the bed, so the officers wouldn't have a clean shot.

They were on the fourth floor, so jumping wasn't an option. But as she ran, Anna snatched the IV pole and speared it through the glass. She then turned it sideways, both sides locking on either side of the wall as she jumped through the window.

The IV pole caught on the wall, giving her essentially a chin-up bar to hold onto as she fell out the window.

She then swung out and back against the hospital wall with the same momentum, kicking once, twice.

The window below was almost out of reach. But the very top of the glass gave way to her kicking.

The security guards leaned out of Malcolm's window nearly on her, but she dropped, catching the next ledge below and muscling through the now open window on the third floor.

Inside this hospital room, an old man was unconscious in a bed. A nurse was standing there, fingers frozen on an IV drip as she looked in shock at the broken window, screaming as Anna darted past.

"Sorry, ma'am," Anna said breathlessly as she bolted into the hall, double-timing it.

The security guards were still on the floor above, and her path to the exit stairwell was clear. She kept running, though, and her mind tried to keep up.

A biker bar outside Mammoth Lakes... A gang who'd paid off a cop then tried to kill him.

What had Beth got herself involved in? Why take Beth and her family? Was her sister still alive? She took the stairs three at a time, her jaw set as she raced towards the exit.

Chapter 12

She came to slowly... and in pain.

Beth's body ached as the coarse ropes dug into her wrists and ankles, leaving marks on her once-smooth skin. The damp basement air filled her lungs with each shallow breath, amplifying the urgency of her situation. She wriggled uncomfortably in the wooden chair, her muscles strained from lack of movement.

Where was she?

Horrible memories returned of the previous night. Terror welled within her.

Her instinct was to pull on the ropes binding her, but instead she froze, taking a breath. Beth recalled Anna had once told her about an escape she'd once made... She'd said if you're tied up, don't pull on the ropes, because you'll only make the knots tighter. Instead... Instead... Beth groaned, blinking back tears.

She couldn't remember what her sister had said now and the lost memory made her want to burst into tears.

Anna would've known exactly what to do. Beth didn't have a clue.

She closed her eyes, taking a long, full breath through her nose. Ok, Beth... Calm. Calm, she told herself. What had Anna said?

Small circles.

Beth's eyes shot open. That was it. You have to move your wrists in small circles to loosen the knots over time. She closed her eyes and focused on her sister's advice, she worked her wrists in tiny movements.

The friction of the coarse rope on her wrists felt like miniature saw blades, and the repetitive movement sent a sensation through her like she was cutting off her hands a millimeter at a time. Beth blinked and felt a hot tear streak on her cheek, but she stiffened her lip, using every ounce of courage and determination within her to endure the pain.

With each passing minute feeling like an eternity, Beth refused to stop. Time was precious, and she had no idea how much she might have. The lives of her loved ones depended on her resolve. Where was Tom? Where was little Tony? Where was Sarah?

Pushing through the pain, Beth could feel the knot slowly giving way.

The dark, dank room was empty save for her bound form. No furniture. Just a bare, unfinished room.

A basement? Some sort of cellar or storage unit?

Beth gritted her teeth, the pain in her wrists intensifying as she twisted them against the harsh ropes. Sweat dripped down her brow, her focus unwavering. "Think of the kids," she whispered, using their faces to fuel her efforts. Her hands throbbed with every small movement, but she couldn't afford to falter.

Her voice trembled, barely audible in the stale basement air. She couldn't let thoughts of her children's terror paralyze her. They needed her now more than ever.

God, where is Tom? Panic bubbled within her chest, threatening to choke her. The unfamiliar room spun around her, dimly lit and filled with shadows that seemed to close in on her, suffocating her. She took deep breaths through clenched teeth. Beth scanned the basement, trying to piece together what had happened. Dust lined the walls, and the damp floor was cold beneath her feet. Her husband could be anywhere—hurt, or worse. The thought sent a shudder down her spine. She wasn't able to push her emotions away like her big sister... Anna always knew what to do.

"Come on, come on," she muttered under her breath, the rope biting into her raw skin. She winced but kept going, driven by the desperate need to save her family.

Finally, she felt the knot give way, and tears pricked the corners of her eyes. "I did it," she whispered, cradling her bruised wrist, the tender, red rash of friction burns making her hands tremble. But there was no time for celebration or self-pity; she had to find Tom and the children before their captors returned.

She pushed from her chair, squeezing at her raw wrists and holding back her desire to scream.

She needed to stay strong.

"Tony? Sarah?" Beth whispered, her voice trembling as she strained to hear any hint of her children. Every nerve in her body was on high alert, and the silence around her felt oppressive, smothering.

"Mom?" A faint, frightened reply came from behind a door further down the dark room. Relief washed over Beth like a warm wave.

She hastened towards the door and tried the handle.

Locked.

"Tom? Are you in there?"

"Daddy's not here," whispered little Tony.

"Okay, Tony, listen, just stay calm, alright. Is Sarah there with you?"

"Yes," came Sarah's small voice.

The thought of her three and five-year-old locked in the dark filled her with dread and rage.

"Listen to me, both of you." Beth kept her voice low, but her tone firm. "Stay calm. Stay quiet. I'll get us out of here, I promise." Her heart clenched at the thought of her children so terrified, yet she forced herself to sound confident, strong—for their sake.

"Okay, Mom," Tony whispered back, his words barely audible. Sarah's quiet sniffle followed, and Beth imagined her daughter nodding, eyes wide with fear.

"Good. I love you both so much," Beth murmured, her resolve steeling against the pain in her wrist and the unknown dangers that lurked nearby.

Suddenly, the faint sound of murmurs from the room above reached her ears, sending icy tendrils of dread coursing through her veins. The voices were muffled, indistinct, but one thing was clear: their captors were still close.

"Mom, I'm scared," Sarah whimpered, her voice trembling like a leaf in the wind.

"Shh, honey," Beth soothed, taking a shaky breath to steady her own racing heart. "Remember our hiding game? Pretend this is just another round. You're both so good at it, and I'll find you soon."

"Okay," Tony whispered again, his voice steadier than before. Beth could sense his determination to protect his little sister, even through the thick wooden door that separated them. It filled her with a fierce, almost primal pride.

"Stay strong," she whispered back, fighting to keep her own fear at bay. "I'm coming."

As the footsteps overhead grew louder, Beth knew she needed to act fast.

With a quick glance around the dimly lit basement, Beth's eyes darted from corner to corner, searching for anything that could help her break through the door. A wave of despair threatened to overcome her as she realized the room was nearly empty, save for the chair she had been tied to and a few scattered bits of debris. Time was running out; she could feel it in the hollow pit of her stomach.

"Think, think," she muttered under her breath, fighting back the tears that threatened to spill over. She couldn't afford to lose control now, not when her children were depending on her.

Her gaze fell upon a rusty pipe lying in the shadows, half-buried in shadow. It wasn't much, but it was the best chance she had. Ignoring the pain in her wrists, she stumbled forward and grasped the cold metal with shaking hands.

"Mom, are you still there?" Tony's voice whispered through the crack beneath the door, trembling with anxiety.

"Stay quiet, sweetheart," she replied, forcing herself to sound calm and collected despite the panic gnawing at her insides. "I'm going to try to get this door open."

"Be careful, Mom," Tony said, his voice barely audible. The fear in his voice only fueled Beth's determination to get them all out of this nightmare.

"Always am, honey," she whispered back, giving the door one last look. This had to work – there was no other option.

Beth lifted the pipe above her head and brought it down hard against the door, the impact reverberating through her entire body. She winced at the pain shooting up her arm but continued, each strike more frantic than the last.

"Come on, come on," she muttered, desperation clawing at her chest as she threw every ounce of strength she had left into breaking through to her children. The door began to splinter, but it wasn't enough. She needed more time—time she didn't have.

The footsteps overhead suddenly stopped, and the murmurs from the room above grew ominously silent. Her heart pounded in her chest like a caged animal, and she knew, without a doubt, that they were coming for her.

"Mom?" Tony whispered, his voice shaking with terror.

"Keep quiet, I'll handle this," she assured him, her own voice barely audible as she gripped the pipe tightly, prepared to face whatever danger awaited.

The sound of heavy footsteps descending the stairs echoed through the basement, growing louder and closer with each passing second.

Chapter 13

Anna approached the biker bar, a scowl on her face. She adjusted the bandage wrapped around her thigh into a more comfortable position. Only a faint tinge of red from the barbed wire wound showed through; this was partly from the cuts beginning to clot, but also because of the double-thick wrapping of gauze that Anna used to conceal a knife against her leg.

The biker bar, under the cover of midnight, didn't look to have received the memo about the late hour. Neon lights flashed into the dimly lit streets, casting an eerie glow on the worn-out facade of the bar. The sound of revving engines and raucous laughter spilled out into the night.

Anna scanned the bikes lined outside the front of the joint. The chromed bodies glistened under the kaleidoscope of flickering colors, each with its own distinct personality, custom paint jobs, and modifications that implied their unspoken road stories, none of them particularly polite.

Anna's eyes were drawn to a black Harley-Davidson, its sleek frame exuding an undeniable power. Its handlebars rose like outstretched wings. Beside it stood a vintage Triumph Bonneville, its classic lines harkening back to a time of rebellion and rock 'n' roll. The sun-faded blue paint hinted at countless adventures taken on winding country roads.

She had never owned a bike herself, but enough members on the team had, leaving her an appreciation for the machines.

But now... they were going to be a useful tool.

She started checking the fuel caps, moving swiftly, and glancing towards the closed door to the bar to make sure no one spotted her.

No security cameras here. In a place like this, surveillance was unwelcome.

She grabbed the plastic cap on the Harley and unscrewed it, the scent of fuel hitting her nose like bad moonshine. Glancing around, Anna spotted an old bandana, worn from sweat and washed blood, tied to one of the handlebars.

She snatched the cloth, dipped it in the fuel tank, then, the acrid scent of gasoline lingering on the air, she draped it down the side.

An insurance policy.

She left the bike that way and approached the door to the bar.

Anna pushed open the creaky wooden door and stepped inside. The atmosphere hit her like a wave: a concoction of sweat, cigarette smoke, and cheap whiskey. She scanned the room, her eyes locking onto a group of burly bikers huddled together at the far end of the bar.

As she made her way through the crowd, Anna couldn't help but notice the curious gazes that followed her every move. She was a sight to behold—a woman unafraid to venture into this den of testosterone-fueled aggression.

There were a scant few women in this place, though the ones present were also mean mugging her. She decided a tactful approach wasn't going to work.

Someone here had hired Malcolm Davis as a getaway driver. Someone here was involved in her sister's disappearance. She'd had enough of skulking around mansions.

Now, she wanted answers. She stomped straight towards the huddle of large bikers.

She could feel their eyes boring into her, sizing her up with their predatory gaze. The leader of the pack, a towering man with a scruffy beard and tattoos snaking up his arms, finally broke the silence.

"What's a pretty thing like you doing in a place like this?" he asked, lips curling into a sly grin.

"I'm looking for someone," she replied coolly.

The biker gang exchanged glances, their expressions filled with curiosity and suspicion.

"I'm not a cop," she added.

This would remove a veneer of protection, but it also might shake things up a bit more.

The big biker leaned forward, jutting out a finger and tapping her shoulder. "This is a members-only club, lady. You should get out while you can."

She looked down at the finger then up again.

She didn't move. Didn't react.

She just waited patiently. "Which of you was involved with Malcolm Davis?"

She was studying the faces and trying to see if she recognized any of them from Davis' mansion. But they were unfamiliar to her.

Los Hermanos had far fewer Hispanic members than she'd anticipated, given the name. But the leader in question was a tanned fellow with dark eyes. His gaze fixated on her like a needle pinning butterfly wings to a collection book.

"Who's Malcolm Davis?"

"A cop. Corrupt cop. Were you the one paying him?" she said, without missing a beat.

Direct. This time, she was going to be direct.

A few voices could be heard coming from a backroom. her eyes glanced down the long hall, and she spotted a sliver of light emanating from a door.

"None of your business what's that way," snapped the large biker, stepping to block her view.

"Now I definitely want to know what's back there," she replied.

"Think you're cute?"

"No. Pissed off. Touch me again, and I take your finger home with me."

GUARDIAN'S VENGEANCE

A couple of the other bikers, clearly drunk, chuckled at this. One of them took a long gulp of beer then burped in her face. Another flashed a knife, twirling it between tattooed knuckles.

"Think you might be lost, senorita," he said.

Anna just watched them coldly. She needed to find out how the Los Hermanos were involved in her sister's disappearance. She couldn't imagine why straight-laced Beth would assosciate with anyone in this biker's bar. It was something she'd always been jealous about with Beth. Her sister was simply... good.

She did the right thing for the right reasons. Anna, on the other hand, felt as if she often had to bend rules just to fulfill a mission.

And now... she was considering all sorts of things to bend as she faced the leather-clad, overly tattooed men. She took a step back as one drew closer to her—not out of fear, but out of a desire to maintain distance.

She still hadn't decided if she was going to drive a thumb through his left eye if he tried to grab at her again, and when faced with a group, it was always best to maintain combat distance.

But before she could react, she spotted movement in the back of the bar.

Behind a wooden, bead curtain, a man was frowning in her direction. He stood in the shadows of the wooden drapes, watching her speculatively. A few seconds later, he pulled out a phone, and turned, rattling something off in Spanish she didn't understand.

She frowned in his direction.

"Hey... I'm talking to you girlie," one of the smelliest and largest of the bikers was saying. He reached out to poke her again, and this time she caught his finger, twisted it, and swept his leg.

The move was so fast that if someone blinked, they would've missed it.

The biker let out a yelp of pain as he crashed to the floor, clutching his injured hand. The other men stopped laughing and taunting, their expressions turning from amusement to surprise. Anna stood tall, her gaze never wavering from the man behind the bead curtain.

"Pardon me," she said softly, and she brushed between two of the bikers. They shuffled back, surprise still etched on their features.

The man behind the bead curtain was moving now, phone still pressed to his face. He didn't glance back, but she had the distinct impression he knew she was there. Was he trying to lure her? She hesitated, a frown creasing her features. Was she being drawn into something? She'd entered the bar unarmed, save the knife in the thigh strap. But a knife in her hand was more effective than most weapons. Especially in such close proximity.

She shot a look towards where the bikers were glaring after her, their eyes narrowed into mean slits.

She stepped under the bead curtains, which rattled around her. The air inside the dimly lit room was heavy with a mixture of cigarette smoke and anticipation. Anna's eyes adjusted to the change in lighting as she made her way through the narrow corridor beyond the bead curtains. The walls were adorned with faded posters of rock bands and provocative pin-up girls, adding an element of grit to the atmosphere.

At first, Anna was prepared for some of the bikers to follow her, to try to stop her from going through the bead curtain, but as none of them did, a more chilling idea occurred to her.

Whatever was back here intimidated the bikers too.

Sounds of malicious laughter and raucous conversation steadily rose from the main bar once more, gradually fading away as Anna ventured deeper into the heart of the building.

The man ahead of her kept pacing hurriedly, without glancing back.

She couldn't shake off the feeling that she was being watched, scrutinized by unseen eyes hiding within the shadows of the building's surprisingly honeycombed back halls. There was more back here than she'd expected, and the shadowy offshoots of halls and dark rooms felt like some monster's cave from a fairy-tale.

After a few short turns, the hall ended in a doorway. The man on the cell phone was nowhere to be seen, but there was nowhere else he could have gone, she hadn't been *that* far behind him. Over the door, she spotted two cameras looking down like eyes over the mouth of the closed door.

The air seemed to grow colder, causing goosebumps to rise on her skin. But there was nothing for it. Whatever answers could be found, would be through here. She was certain of it.

Trusting her instincts, Anna freed the concealed knife from the bandage on her thigh and held it in a backward grip, keeping it palmed and the blade hidden behind her forearm.

Stepping through the door, the atmosphere shifted as Anna entered a dimly lit storehouse. The odd, maze-like mess of corridors suddenly made more sense. The bar had been attached to the adjoining building, a large and likely intentionally abandoned-looking warehouse. The air was thick with the scent of motor oil and burnt rubber.

The walls were lined with shelves, filled to the brim with spare parts and tools. Dust danced in the rays of moonlight that streamed through cracks in the walls, giving the space an ethereal glow. Each step sent a low vibration through the concrete floor, reminding Anna that she was an intruder.

Anna's eyes caught movement and locked onto the man she'd followed, still engrossed in his phone conversation.

They were alone, and she was tired of waiting her turn to chat.

"Who are you?" she called out suddenly.

The man turned slowly, studying her. His eyebrow quirked up.

She approached him, a scowl on her features. "I said who are you?"

He was still holding the phone, but no longer talking. He just watched her. Finally, he switched from Spanish to English flawlessly, betraying no accent to hint which was his native tongue. "I have proof of life," he said simply.

She blinked, staring at him.

Her hand was tight around the handle of her hidden knife. She kept it raised behind her forearm.

He watched her, waiting.

"My sister?" Anna said.

"You are Anna Gabriel, yes?"

She frowned. "Who's asking?"

"Just a messenger."

She felt a slow chill down her spine. How did this man know her name? Why did it seem as if he'd been expecting her? As if he'd been waiting for her to show up. What the hell was going on here?

She felt another chill and glanced back towards the door leading out of the warehouse and back to the backroom corridors of the bar.

It remained empty.

They both remained alone... For now.

"I don't know what you want," she said quietly. "But I need a name."

"John," he said simply. "You can call me John. Would you like proof of life?" He extended the phone to her again.

She stared at him, distrust etched into her features, her hand clutching her knife tightly. She felt as if she were in a play without her lines. Someone had known she was coming. But how? Who was this guy?

There were too many unknowns, too many unanswered questions. She had always been meticulous in her planning, but now she found herself standing in an unfamiliar territory, caught off guard and vulnerable.

With a mix of curiosity and caution, Anna reached out and took the phone from John's outstretched hand. She examined the screen, her heart pounding in her chest. It was a phone call, and the device was connected to an external line.

She frowned hesitantly, glancing at John. "Who is this?"

"Your brother-in-law," he said simply.

She raised the phone. "Tom?"

"Anna!" the voice said on the other end, urgent and desperate. "Oh, thank God. Anna! Are you okay?"

"Tom?" she snapped, "What's going on?"

But suddenly, the line went dead.

She stared. "What did you do?" she said, her voice cold.

"Nothing," John replied. "I don't control the other phone."

She tried redialing the number, but it went straight to voicemail. Her anger was mounting now. Hearing her brother-in-law's familiar voice had only further infuriated her.

"Where's Beth?" she snarled, clutching the phone tightly.

"I couldn't say," John replied softly.

The moonlight streamed through the window, illuminating his plain, olive-skinned features. He looked like a banker more than a biker, and he watched her from behind hooded eyes.

"What have you done to her?" Anna demanded, her voice trembling with a mixture of fear and fury. "Where is she?"

John held up his hands in a placating gesture. "I haven't harmed her," he assured her calmly. "But I can't say the same for Los Hermanos."

Hearing those words sent a chill down Anna's spine. They were notorious for their involvement in illegal activities—drug trafficking, arms smuggling—the list went on. But kidnapping? Murder?

"Why are Los Hermanos after my sister?" Anna asked, trying to keep her voice steady.

"You are asking the wrong questions," John said quietly. "You heard his voice..."

"Tom's, yeah. I want to hear Beth."

"She is alive. So are the two little ones," he said, speaking matter-of-factly as if he were commenting on the weather. "Now you should be asking better questions."

She resisted the urge to lash out and choke him. "What questions are those?"

He sniffed. "How you can get them back, Anna Gabriel."

"You knew I was coming. That we'd be here, talking like this. How?" she snapped.

"We know the information of everyone we do business with," he said quietly.

She snorted. "I haven't done business with..." she trailed off. "Beth? Beth wouldn't have gone to you. Don't lie to me."

He shrugged. "I haven't lied."

She frowned at the phone clutched in her hand. "Where are they?" she said.

"I don't know."

"I said where are they?" she demanded, her voice tense. The rest of her body followed suit. At any moment, she was poised to lunge at the plain-faced, blinking man.

She noticed now just how often he seemed to blink, his eyes constantly shuttering like camera lenses. Was he nervous? Likely.

But they were alone. In this old, worn warehouse behind the biker's bar, they were alone. Did he think he could overpower her? Had he called in backup?

Her confusion was mounting, and so she tried to focus on her training. Preparation was often key to victory, but even in the best-laid ops, sometimes improvisation was key. Right now, she didn't have control of the room, but that could change.

"I don't know where they are," he said, more firmly.

She darted forward. One moment, she'd been standing still and quiet, and the next, she lunged forward, knife in hand. She pressed it to his neck while simultaneously gouging her knee into his midriff. He doubled over with a gasp, and she sent him clattering to the ground, with her on top.

She put the knife against his throat, pressing him to the floor. "I said, where are they?"

He blinked at her, swallowed nervously, but—head still resting on cold concrete—he said, "I really, truly, don't know."

Anna felt her anger intensify at his response. She pressed the knife harder against his throat, a drop of blood trickling down his skin.

"You better start giving me some answers," she threatened, her voice laced with venom.

John's eyes widened, fear flickering in his gaze. "I swear, Ms. Gabriel, I don't have all the details. But I know how you can get them back?"

"Why would Los Hermanos target my sister?" she asked, her grip on the knife tightening. He didn't answer, so she snapped, "So how do I get them back?"

John coughed, struggling for breath under Anna's weight. He wasn't a threat. He wasn't secretly armed. A herd of muscle-bound gunmen didn't come bursting through the door, though, she kept checking entry points.

This strange man with the blinking eyes had come alone... If he really knew who she was, he wouldn't have done this.

Unless...

It hadn't been his call.

If he was just a pawn, then someone had sent him into her clutches.

To deliver the demands...

Who would be so callous with an underling? This wasn't a biker... he didn't have the look.

"Two million dollars," he said simply.

She hesitated, her hand still tight on her knife. "What?"

He swallowed, but then winced, not wanting to move his throat. "That is what you're required to pay. For each of them."

"For each..."

"Beth, Tom, Tony, and Sarah," he rattled off, still somehow keeping his tone even while laying on the concrete floor with a knife pressed to his throat. A grease stain was seeping through his sleeve, but he ignored it.

She snorted. "You've got the wrong girl if you think I have access to that kind of cash."

"I'm aware you don't," he said softly. "But the money that was stolen? We want it back, with interest."

"Stolen? Who stole money?"

He glared at her. "He told us who you are, Anna. Did you really think you'd scare us? We know about your background.

We don't care. If you want to see them alive again, you'll repay everything you stole."

Now, she was flat-out confused. She didn't reply at first, though, preferring to process what she was being told.

The man was speaking adamantly, confidently. Now, he seemed to have lost some of his veneer of fear. He glared up at her, a challenge lingering in his gaze.

"I didn't steal anything from you."

"We know you're in on it," snapped the man. "If you want them alive, you need to return all of it."

She paused briefly. Beth was a stay-at-home mom. This was something that had caused her sister embarrassment in the past, whenever the two of them emailed, but Anna had always told her sister she wished she could've traded jobs.

And Anna meant it.

She killed people for a living. She'd gone off to war with romantic notions of what it would entail. Testing her own resolve was reward enough, at some points. But over time, a tested will was secondary to the mission.

The idea of coming home to a loving family, in a safe neighborhood... Or what should've been a safe neighborhood. Her heart panged. She envied her little sister. She wished she'd told Beth this more often.

But now, she was stuck. The man thought she had money she didn't have. It had been years since she'd seen her baby sister in person.

The idea that Beth was some sort of thief was laughable but how well did she really know her baby sister?

She shook her head.

No... no they'd grown up together.

Beth was the sort to apologize if she ate someone's leftover pizza. Beth wasn't a thief. But this man seemed to think Anna had access to the money.

If he knew she didn't, chances were things wouldn't go well for her... or Beth's family.

So she didn't deny it a second time. Instead, she said, "How am I supposed to get the money to you."

His eyes shone as he stared at her, still laying in that grease puddle on the ground.

"We have a rendezvous. You give us the money, and we'll return your family."

"Fat chance," she retorted. "You return my family and then you get your money."

He snorted.

She pressed her knife again.

He gasped but shook his head. "If you kill me, they'll just send another."

"Who's they?" she snapped.

"It's worth more than my skin to tell you."

She lifted the knife and stood to her feet suddenly, glaring down at the man. She'd heard a noise.

The sound was coming from the parking lot to their right. She glanced towards the lot, visible through the floor-to-ceiling window.

A jeep had pulled into the lot. Shadows were emerging.

She stared, her spine stiffening as she realized men with guns were rising from the back of the jeep.

Chapter 14

Anna's heart pounded as she spotted the gunmen emerging from the Jeep, visible through the smudged window.

"You called for help?" she asked, quirking an eyebrow.

The man who'd provided his name as "John" glanced over and tensed.

"Shoulda told them to park elsewhere," she muttered. She was glaring down at the man now. "You want to live?" she said. "Tell me where the rendezvous is."

"Bring us the money," he snapped.

"Where do we meet?"

"I'll message you," he replied.

The back door suddenly banged open. She heard loud voices. Boots thumping against the concrete.

He shrugged at her. "Boss is an impatient man. You should've moved faster. Now..." he shook his head. "They'll make you tell them where the money is."

Anna didn't listen, she was already turning on her heel.

She spotted multiple figures in bulletproof vests emerging from behind a stack of shipping crates and old vehicle parts. They were carrying semi-automatic rifles on shoulder straps. She spotted more than one grenade in a bandolier. She was already moving, though. She hit the lights on the wall as she ran, dousing the place in darkness.

The men with the guns cursed. The chatter of bullets erupted in the quiet, dusty warehouse.

Anna sprinted through the darkness. The gunfire echoed around her, ricocheting off the walls of the warehouse. She could hear the men shouting, trying to locate her as she stuck to the shadows, moving behind a concrete support beam and bee-lining back to the bead curtain.

She had more questions now than when she'd first entered this place.

But it wasn't time to naval gaze.

He would text her the location of the rendezvous. She wouldn't show up with the money. How could she? But she'd get her family back one way or another. What had Beth gotten herself into?

Anna weaved through stacks of crates and rusty machinery, evading the armed men as they blindly fired their weapons. She relied on her instincts, her honed skills as a trained assassin guiding her every move.

As Anna neared an exit, she heard heavy footsteps approaching from behind. Without hesitation, she ducked into a small alcove and pressed herself against the wall, holding her breath. An armed man passed by, moving slowly, rifle raised. A flashlight attachment sent a beam across the wall. She allowed him to pass, holding incredibly still.

Once he was gone, Anna pushed herself off the wall and continued forward, careful to remain silent. She spotted him five paces ahead, and then slipped down the left side of the room, away from the bead curtain and this time towards an open window.

Two more gunmen were shouting directives at the others. She heard the gasping voice of "John" as he said, "She was just here. She's armed with a knife."

The weasel was still talking, but she could no longer hear him as she sprinted towards the open window. Ten feet. Five.

Suddenly, a burst of illumination off to her left as another salvo of gunfire tore through the warehouse. The window shattered. Bullets whizzed by her skin. She flung herself through the window, rolling in the grass outside, and sending up a geyser of shattered glass. In the same motion, she reached her feet and kept running, the gunmen in hot pursuit.

She needed a distraction. Something to cover her retreat. And she spotted it.

The gasoline rag she'd left in the tank of the nearest Harley.

"Sorry," she muttered under her breath, hoping that this bike belonged to Mr. Pokey from inside the bar. She stumbled towards it, pulled a lighter, lit the rag, and then bolted around the side of the bar.

The gasoline-soaked rag erupted in flames, and the fire spread down the rag, into the gas tank.

The explosion echoed through the night as Anna dove behind a dumpster, shielded from the blast. Flames licked the air, casting an orange glow across the deserted parking lot. The gunmen halted in their pursuit, momentarily stunned by the sudden chaos.

Taking advantage of the distraction, Anna hastened away into the darkness, under the smoke, racing back towards where she'd parked her RV; her heart pounding in her chest.

She slipped into the driver's seat, gunned the engine, and roared out of the parking lot. Only now, as she sped along the road, did her mind slowly quiet. She counted to ten in her mind, trying to refocus. What had that all been about?

Los Hermanos were the bikers... so who were the gunmen? And who was "John?"

She shook her head, muttering darkly to herself. Checking her phone, there were no messages. But someone had her sister... someone had her sister's family, and that person wanted two million dollars each for the return of her loved ones.

No matter how much she might want to, there was no way for Anna to pull together eight million. Money didn't matter to her. She'd never thought much of it, and so had rarely accumulated much.

But it was a lead.

These guys were demanding the return of their money, which meant someone had stolen it. She couldn't rule anyone out. Maybe Beth really had somehow been involved. It would've shocked her, but Anna had to admit she hadn't exactly been an older sister of the more proximate type.

As she sped away from the old, biker bar, hitting the highway under the cover of night, her hands tightened on the steering wheel.

"Dummy," she muttered under her breath.

She scowled now, feeling a rising sense of anger.

It was staring her in the face.

Tom was an accountant of sorts. He moved money. She'd always considered him a meek, mild sort of fellow.

Tom was the voice she'd heard on the phone. Tom was their proof of life.

What if Beth hadn't been the target at all? What if Beth had simply been caught in the crossfire?

She knew she couldn't jump to conclusions; she couldn't absolve her baby sister of wrongdoing based on her desire to, but the more she thought about it, the more it made sense. They'd likely gotten her name from emails they'd exchanged.

"Yeah," she whispered to herself.

It was as if she were speaking into the silence of her old RV. The rumbling, souped-up engine provided a comforting background noise. "Tom, what the hell have you been up to?" she muttered.

If Tom had been embezzling money, or shuffling it around for Los Hermanos, it would explain why he'd been taken, along with his family. But just because she had a theory for the cause of this mess didn't mean she had a conclusion to it.

She checked her phone again. Still no point of rendezvous.

If she could find that money, maybe she'd have a bargaining chip. Assuming Tom had stolen it, she'd be able to find it. But she was better at tracking people than money. Her skills were hunting out targets that needed to be taken out, and if she was going to do this, she'd need to think like a thief... an embezzler... a conman...

Then it hit her...

"Waldo," she whispered under her breath.

The career criminal had been sneaking around a burnt-out husk of her sister's home. He'd been sifting through the ash, looking for valuables. She'd found him with the jewelry, hadn't she?

What if he'd been looking for something even more valuable?

What if he'd been involved in all of this?

She scowled now, her teeth set.

She needed to find Waldo Strange the Third. If he was more deeply involved than she'd first thought, then she'd made a terrible mistake by letting him walk the first time.

But how could she find him?

She sighed, realizing now that maybe she'd bitten off more than she could chew.

She nibbled on the corner of her lip, tapping her fingers on the steering wheel as she navigated the night-time roads.

She knew she needed backup. She stared at her phone. She needed to find Waldo, and if there was one person who could help... Her mind shifted to Casper... Casper the friendly Ghost had been the call-sign of a man by the name of Carlos Antoni.

But Casper had long since left the SEALs. Casper was, quite figuratively, a ghost. He worked private security now, and he was one of the only operators from Team Six that she kept in contact with.

Was it worth contacting an old friend for a job like this?

If not now, when?

She pulled up her screen, dialing the number from memory.

As she entered each digit, she felt a rising sense of unease.

Things were all moving so fast. Danger lurked around every corner, and she felt as if she were being backed into a corner by some unseen predator.

She didn't like feeling as if she had her back against a wall. Which was why she needed backup.

She gave a brief nod and pressed call.

The phone rang three times... and then it went dead.

She frowned.

He'd hung up on her.

She tried again, staring at the screen.

This time, the device went straight to voicemail. She shifted uncomfortably. She sent a quick text. "It's me. Anna."

This time, she didn't have to wait long.

Anna who? the message replied.

She scowled.

You know who, asshole. Don't make me say it.

She hated her own call-sign. But the text messages stopped. He hadn't replied. Anna sighed in frustration, then typed, It's Guardian Angel. Anna Gabriel. Now call me.

No sooner had she sent the message then her phone began to vibrate. An incoming call lit up her screen in blue, and with a rising sense of anticipation, she answered the call.

Chapter 15

Midnight was thick across the horizon as Anna Gabriel pulled into the parking lot behind the fast food joint. The scent of burgers and fries hung in the air. She checked her mirror, determining the roads were clear.

She spotted workers still inside the fast-food joint, playing on their phones, or engaging with the errant customer who occasionally meandered through the drive-thru.

She scanned the parking lot and spotted the single sedan with tinted windows in the back of the space.

She pulled her RV up to the sedan, rolling down her window as she drew near.

The sedan's window matched.

A man was sitting in the front seat, tossing a couple of fries into his mouth, and watching her from behind sunglasses.

She stared at Casper.

"Still wearing those at night, huh?" she said, pointing at his sunglasses.

"Still nosing in other peoples' business?" he retorted. He dipped a fry in some ketchup and tossed it in his mouth. He tilted the fries towards her, offering them.

Normally, Anna liked to stick with brown rice and chicken. Now that she was outside the service, she knew that keeping her physique was the only way to make sure she could keep up with her two-a-day-workouts.

Most people worked out to stay trim. She stayed trim so she could workout.

But her stomach rumbled, and she realized it had been all day since she'd had something to eat. Still, she wasn't hungry.

"Nah, thanks," she muttered.

"Suit yourself. More for me." He shoveled a few more fries into his mouth with greasy fingers.

Casper was a bit chubbier than the last time she'd seen him overseas. The two of them had served two tours together on two different continents. He hadn't been there on her third go-around while working black ops, but he had been a steady current in a tumultuous career.

Casper looked like he had settled comfortably into civilian life, his days of intense physical training and combat behind him. But Anna knew better than to underestimate him. Casper may have gained a few pounds, but his eyes still held that sharpness that made him a formidable warrior.

"So, Anna," Casper said between mouthfuls of fries, "what brings you here in the dead of night? Last time I checked, you were off fighting wars and saving the world."

Anna sighed, her eyes searching Casper's face for any sign of doubt or hesitation. "I didn't ask you to drive out," she said. "A phone call would've been fine."

"Can't trust 'em," he replied.

"I believe you."

"Besides," he added, waving a fry, "I live a couple hours down the road. Thought you knew that."

She shook her head. "I didn't. Knew you were local but didn't know it was that local."

Casper wiped the greasy residue from his fingers onto a napkin before meeting Anna's gaze. "You know I owe you one, Anna. So I'm here. What's the problem."

She studied the man. Besides his aging features and his sunglasses at night, he had shaved his head nearly completely.

His scalp gleamed under the dim parking lot lights. It was a stark contrast to the shaggy, blond curls he used to sport during their time in the SEALs. But Anna recognized that this transformation was more than just a physical change. Casper had shed his past self, leaving behind the trappings of war and embracing a new identity.

"The problem," Anna began, her voice heavy with concern, "is Waldo Strange the Third."

Casper's eyebrows shot up. "That a real person or a handle?"

"I don't know. But I need to find him." A car was pulling past them, moving towards the drive-through, so Anna leaned closer, her voice dropping to a whisper. "I think Waldo is involved in something dangerous. And I need your help to find him."

Casper's eyes grew serious as he listened, his fingers unconsciously tapping on the steering wheel. "This guy a threat?"

"I can't say for sure, but my gut tells me there's more to him than meets the eye. I found him in a burnt-out home."

"Huh. Looter?"

"Probably. It was my sister's home."

Casper let out a low whistle, running his hand over his shaved head. "Shit. Sorry. She's here?"

"I don't know where she is," Anna said, tight-lipped.

He clicked his tongue, shaking his head side to side. "Not good. Alright... so let's say I trade ya."

"Okay..." she said cautiously. "What's the trade?"

"I help you locate this Waldo character, and anything else you need..."

"As long as we're making a shopping list, I need you to find eight million dollars."

His eyebrows perked up behind his shades again.

"Eight..." he trailed off.

"You're good with computers still, right? Or you lost that touch too?"

"What do you mean too?" he demanded, pointing a greasy finger.

"Nothing," she said quickly. "Just... I need you to track Tom Gabriel's records. He's my sister's husband."

"Gabriel?"

"He took her last name."

"Gotcha. Okay... Not a problem. So if you want me to find Waldo and track Tom's financials... I want something in return."

"I can pay you," she said.

"Settlement still paying out?" he asked.

"You know about that?"

"Only a little. But nah, keep your chump change. I want something else."

She frowned, "Go on."

"I want you to tell me why you were discharged." He leaned forward, staring at her, relishing her sudden discomfort. "No one knows why, Guardian. I talked to Charlie right after we got off the call. He didn't even know you were out."

"I've been out five years," she replied quickly.

"He didn't know."

"Charlie doesn't know anything."

"True. But why were you kicked?" he said.

She shifted uncomfortably in her seat.

She could feel the weight of Casper's stare, penetrating her like a laser beam. The car hummed with anticipation, the tension between them all too apparent. Anna's mind raced, considering her options. She had always been guarded about her past, meticulously crafting a facade that hid the truth of her discharge from the ranks.

"How about this?" Anna finally spoke, her voice steady and firm. "I'll tell you why I was discharged, but only after we find Waldo and figure out what he's been up to."

Casper leaned back in his seat, mulling over her proposition. The rhythmic tapping of his fingers ceased as he considered the offer. "Seems fair enough," he eventually conceded. "But remember, Guardian, I'm not your lackey. I'll help you find Waldo and dig into Tom Gabriel's financials, but you better hold up your end of the bargain."

Anna nodded, a sense of relief washing over her. She had managed to strike a delicate balance in their agreement, albeit at the cost of revealing her deepest secret. She tried to stay tight-lipped. It would make the rounds. Her old teammates, commanders... they'd find out her deepest shame.

She'd intentionally kept it under wraps but in order to help her sister?

She had to do it.

As they continued their conversation in hushed tones, Anna couldn't help but steal quick glances at Casper. His appearance was an enigma in itself – tattooed arms peeking out from beneath his sleeves, a fading jawline accentuated by a five o'clock shadow, and an unblinking gaze hidden behind dark shades.

And yet... there was something oddly comforting about being in Casper's presence again.

Casper extended a hand.

She took it, shaking.

"Deal," she said.

He offered her some more fries.

This time, she snatched one, took a bite of the salty, oily piece of potato, and said, "So... how do we find Waldo and figure out if he helped steal eight million dollars?"

Chapter 16

Anna stood on the hillside, rifle against her shoulder. Casper had provided her with the Baretta. The scope sat comfortably against her cheek, and her eye pressed to the magnifying glass.

She peered down at the familiar weapon. How many times had she looked down the scope of a rifle in the past? To a trained sniper, the weapon was like an appendage. She went through the motions, checking and double-checking every aspect of her setup. The wind direction, the distance to her target, and the stability of her position were all crucial details that she meticulously assessed. As she scanned the area through the scope, she studied the compound below.

"You're sure he's here?"

"His phone's here, so I'm guessing he is," Casper said behind her.

He still smelled of fast food, and his windbreaker was zipped up, holding back the night-time chill. The hours had stretched past midnight, and now, the two of them sat on the mountainside in the dead of night, staring down at the compound below.

Casper groaned and shifted his leg to keep it from falling asleep, and a stray stone rippled away where his heel clipped the rugged ground. Anna shot him a confused look that melted into friendly sarcasm. "Getting rusty? Can't remember the last time I heard our Friendly Ghost give away his position like that."

Giving an almost inaudible chuckle, Casper replied, "I'm sorry. I thought I was retired. My evening plans involved a pizza, a six-pack, and watching a scary movie with my pants off. Instead, I'm dug in on a crumbling mountain spotting a sniper perch with you."

Anna shook her head. "Shut up. You love it."

Casper only snorted in answer as he carefully, and silently, settled in again.

"What is this place?" she asked quietly.

"Belongs to an old drug outfit," said Casper. He had his phone in his hand, and his fingers flew over the screen with practiced precision. He sounded bored as he leaned against a tree, staring down into the valley below.

The frigid wind howled through the trees as Anna and Casper crouched on the side of a mountain in Mammoth Lakes. They were hidden in the shadows, their breaths hanging like ghosts in the air. The moon cast an eerie glow over the landscape, illuminating the run-down compound below them.

Anna pressed her left eye to the rifle scope, her fingers steady on its cold metal frame. Her piercing gaze scanned the scene below, taking in every detail of the dilapidated buildings and makeshift fences.

The compound was riddled with plumes of smoke that rose from the cook labs for meth production. It was a haven for criminal activity, but they were there to find one man in particular—Waldo Strange. As Anna's gaze shifted between the buildings, she noticed the tension in her shoulders and consciously forced herself to relax.

Anna's eye pressed against the rifle scope, her breath steady as she surveyed the decrepit compound below. The sharp scent of the mountain air mingled with a faint chemical odor that wafted up from the meth labs.

"Anything?" Casper whispered, his voice barely audible.

"Armed guards," Anna replied tersely, her eyes flicking between the men patrolling the perimeter. "But no sign of Waldo yet."

"Keep looking," Casper urged. "He has to be here. His phone is pinging this tower."

As Anna scanned the area, she couldn't shake the gnawing feeling in her gut that something was off. She knew Waldo was a slippery target, but he had to be here.

A sudden commotion caught her attention, and she quickly adjusted her scope to focus on the source of the noise. A man emerged from one of the cook labs, sprinting with a suitcase clutched tightly in his hands.

"Got him!" Anna exclaimed, her pulse quickening. "Waldo's on the move!"

"Where?" Casper asked, peering through his own binoculars.

"Southwest corner," she directed. "Damn it," she muttered under her breath, watching as Waldo weaved through the compound, skillfully evading the armed guards. "He's faster than I thought."

Anna watched gunmen in hazmat suits chase after Waldo, emerging from one of the trailers, shouting and pointing in the fleeing man's direction. They fired shots at him, their weapons bright flashes in the darkness. Waldo narrowly managed to duck behind a shed just as bullets thudded into the wood.

"Shit," Anna muttered, her pulse quickening. "He's trapped."

Anna bit her lip, focusing on her breathing as she scanned the scene below. She could feel the weight of the rifle in her hands, and the steady rise and fall of her chest as she breathed. It was a familiar sensation, one that grounded her amidst the chaos unfolding before her eyes.

"Any ideas?" Casper asked, his voice low and tense.

"Working on it," Anna replied, her mind racing with potential strategies. But as she observed the gunmen closing in on Waldo, she knew time was running out.

The mountain air was sharp and cold as Anna's breath formed a mist in front of her face. She could feel the tension in her muscles, like a coiled spring ready to snap.

As the gunmen closed in on Waldo, Anna breathed out slowly, allowing her instincts to guide her. In that split-second, she made her decision. Her finger tightened around the trigger, and the shot rang out—not at the gunman, but at the ground near his feet, kicking up dirt and debris.

But instead of halting his pursuit, the man just looked briefly confused then charged forward, weapon raised, ready to take out Waldo.

With her heart pounding, Anna spotted her chance. As the gunman raised his weapon to shoot Waldo, she took aim at his hand, holding her breath. She didn't *hope* for success. She didn't offer up a prayer. She knew it would hit the moment she pulled the trigger. The gunshot echoed through the night, and the weapon was wrenched from the man's grasp by the force of her shot.

"Argh!" he screamed, his voice faint in the distance, clutching his injured hand. The other gunmen hesitated, glancing around warily, unsure whether to continue their pursuit or seek cover.

Anna coolly watched as Waldo stumbled forward, narrowly avoiding the hail of bullets that followed. She knew she had bought him some time, but it was only a matter of moments before the situation escalated further. He was ducking behind the large gray structure now, keeping low.

Moonlight glinted off the cold metal of Anna's rifle as she lay prone on the mountainside, her breath steady and controlled. Her sharp eyes scanned the chaos unfolding below in the compound, taking in the fear and desperation that gripped Waldo. He clutched the suitcase tightly as he dove into the grass at the base of the large structure.

"Damn it," she muttered under her breath, watching as the remaining gunmen ignored their comrade with the injured hand and continued to chase Waldo. She couldn't let them take him down. He might have the only answers to the missing eight million.

Waldo stumbled again, narrowly dodging a hail of bullets aimed at his back. He pressed into the shadows behind a ventilation unit outside the main building. He was running out of time and space, the gunmen closing in on him like a pack of hungry wolves. The sound of gunfire punctuated the night air, echoing through the desolate landscape.

"Come on," she urged herself silently, her left eye squinting through the scope. Every second counted, and Anna knew that if she hesitated now, it would be too late.

"Three hundred yards... dark conditions... wind from the west," she thought, calculating the variables and adjusting her aim accordingly. As one of the gunmen raised his weapon to finish Waldo off, she saw her opportunity.

"Shit," she whispered, squeezing the trigger with precision. An instant later, the shot rang out, and the bullet found its mark—right in the gunman's chest. He crumpled to the ground as his comrades faltered in shock.

"Come on, Waldo," Anna whispered, urging him forward as he scrambled to find cover. "Keep moving."

The remaining two gunmen exchanged a glance, their fear obvious even from this distance. They turned on their heels and sprinted away, abandoning their pursuit of their target.

"Looks like they got the message," Casper remarked, his voice still somewhat reserved.

"Yeah," Anna said, her eyes tracking Waldo as he cowered behind the warehouse, tightly clutching the suitcase to his chest.

"Call him," she instructed, her voice cold and focused. She needed to make sure Waldo understood that there was no time to waste. If they didn't get him out of there soon, more gunmen would come.

"Alright," Casper said, pulling out his phone and dialing Waldo's number. "You better pick up, you slippery bastard."

Anna could hear the phone ringing through Casper's speaker, each ring amplifying the tension in the air. Her heart hammered in her chest as she kept her scope trained on Waldo, prepared to take down anyone who threatened him.

"Hello?" Waldo answered, his voice barely audible over the sound of his own panicked breathing.

"Listen up, Waldo," Casper said, his voice steady despite the situation. "You don't know me, but I'm with Anna."

"What? Who's that?"

"Anna Gabriel?" Casper said hesitantly.

"Oh, shit. The crazy lady who scowls a lot?"

Casper glanced at Anna, then back at the phone. "Yeah. That's her."

And resisted the urge to kick out at her old SEAL buddy.

"Look," Casper said, "Anna's got your back, but we need you to move. Now."

"Are you kidding me?" Waldo shot back, his sarcasm an ill-fitting mask for his terror. "I've got bullets flying at me, and you want me to go for a stroll?"

"Unless you want to die here, I suggest you listen," Anna interjected, her voice leaving no room for argument.

"I don't trust you!" he retorted.

"Compare trust," she shot back. "Less or more than the guys trying to kill you?"

"More than I trust those trigger-happy assholes, I guess," Waldo muttered, still gripping the suitcase as if it were a lifeline.

"Then move," she ordered. "We'll guide you."

"Alright, alright," Waldo conceded, gathering his courage. "Here goes nothing."

As Waldo scrambled from his hiding place, Anna kept a watchful eye on every potential danger. She knew that the slightest misstep could mean death.

"Head toward the tree line," Anna instructed, her voice low and cold. "And don't you dare run, or I'll shoot you myself."

"Aw, come on now, you know how much I love your threats," Waldo quipped, his voice shaking despite his attempt at humor.

"Shut up and move, Waldo." She watched him shuffle out from behind the shed, his eyes darting around in search of any remaining gunmen.

Anna's finger twitched on the trigger as she saw Waldo inch closer to safety. The weight of the rifle felt familiar in her hands, the same way it had during all those years of service.

"Almost there, smartass," she muttered, more to herself than Waldo.

"Hey, watch it!" Waldo yelped suddenly as a stray bullet whizzed past him. He stumbled, clutching the suitcase tighter.

"Keep moving!" Anna barked, adrenaline surging through her veins. She shifted her focus, searching for the source of the shot. In a split second, her left eye narrowed and she fired a round towards a balcony just above Waldo's warehouse hiding spot. The sharp crack of the gunshot pierced the air, and the perpetrator slumped to the ground, clutching their shoulder in pain.

"Keep moving," she snapped towards the phone in Casper's hand.

But Waldo had gone still, staying low, breathing heavily. He didn't see the two other drug dealers now emerging from a car in the parking lot behind the cook labs.

They'd see him soon enough.

"Waldo, move!" she snapped.

But he seemed glued to the ground, shaking his head and muttering to himself. "Shit... shit... no. They won't see me," he whispered. "Just... just give me a second."

"Waldo, they're almost on you. I can see them. Move now!"

But he still hesitated, so she acted first.

She fired another shot that struck the suitcase, sending it flying from Waldo's grasp.

"What the hell" Waldo cursed, ducking instinctively.

Anna's keen eyes caught a glimpse of something unusual in the night air. Curiosity piqued, she followed the movement through her scope and was taken aback by what she saw—fluttering bills, illuminated by the faint moonlight, drifting aimlessly as they fell to the ground from where she'd shot the suitcase.

"Son of a bitch," Anna muttered under her breath. "Casper, he's got a case of money."

"Money? You sure?" Casper asked, his voice tense with anticipation. He had been observing the scene from behind binoculars but hadn't noticed the cash.

"Positive," Anna replied, her eyes still locked onto the floating bills. "No wonder they're so hell-bent on catching him. Waldo, you still there?"

"Unfortunately," Waldo huffed, still clutching his ruined suitcase.

"Listen up," Anna commanded, her tone brooking no argument. "You've got about five seconds before they find you. Hear me? Run. Now!"

Waldo grumbled, though Anna could practically hear the wheels turning in his head as he thought of ways to get away again.

The two men from the parking lot had nearly arrived now, both of them holding their weapons tightly as they drew closer.

"Up the hill, towards the large mossy rock," she said quickly.

Waldo adjusted his direction, sprinting away from the drug compound.

Now, the gunmen below seemed to have lost sight of him in the dark. Anna kept her eye on him through her scope until he reached the plateau where the two of them were waiting.

She lowered her rifle then and rose to her feet.

Waldo looked furious as he stumbled over a couple of roots, then regained his footing and marched towards her.

"What the actual hell?" he demanded. "Why'd you shoot the money! I worked hard for that!"

He came within two feet of her, a fist raised, though he didn't look like he knew what to do with it.

Still, she took no chances.

As he closed in, she drove her own fist into his gut. Waldo let out a sound like a whoopee cushion and doubled over, gasping at the ground. She then pulled him up, gripping him by the neck and glaring at him.

"What do you know about eight million missing?" she snapped.

He stared at her, blinking a couple of times. The fear in his eyes was slowly replaced by a dawning horror. He cleared his throat. "Wh-what?"

She shoved him towards the car, still holding the back of his neck. Casper was already sliding into the front seat. He gunned the engine.

"H-hang on," Waldo stammered. "I thought we were done. Where are you taking me?"

She shoved him into the back of the car. Then she joined him. He tried to slide out the other side, but she reached across, locking the door and twisting his wrist. He yelped in pain as Casper gunned the engine. Anna's rifle slipped into the front seat, and Casper pulled away from their lookout spot, moving along the side of the mountain and picking up speed.

Waldo stared forlorn at the locks to the car as if trying to will them open but Anna snatched his chin, turning him to face her. She looked him dead in the eyes.

"Eight mil. Start talking," she demanded, her voice gruff.

He swallowed hesitantly, stammered, then said. "I... I really don't know what you're talking about."

"Try again."

"I don't!" he protested.

"I see... so you're of no use, huh?"

"No! Probably should just let me leave," he said quickly.

"Good call."

He looked briefly relieved until she opened the door while the car was still moving. She began to push him towards the open door.

"What the hell! HEY! HEY! Cut that out!"

Waldo squawked like a bird, fighting desperately to remain in the vehicle as Anna pressed harder, using her well-honed strength to force Waldo closer to the open door.

Casper glanced over at the chaotic scene unfolding in the backseat. "Careful on the leather!" he snapped.

"What are you doing?" Waldo shouted, struggling to keep his seat as the winding mountain road whipped past in a blur just behind him.

Anna gritted her teeth and exerted more force, her grip on Waldo's wrist tightening. As they continued to speed along, she saw fear in his eyes melting into the realization that she was serious about pushing him out of the moving car.

"Okay, okay!" he rattled off. "Holy shit. Just... I swear, I'll talk! Just shut the damn door!" Waldo pleaded, his voice trembling with panic. His hands and feet were splayed, braced against the door.

But she left the door wide. Wind sweeping through in a howl.

"Talk," Anna demanded sternly, her tone leaving no room for negotiation.

The fear of being pushed out of a moving car seemed to override any sort of financial self-preservation.

"I didn't take the money, but I know who did. Okay? I know exactly who did."

"Who?" she snapped.

"You... you can't kill the messenger."

"Who?" she repeated, more firmly.

He swallowed, stared at her, then said, "Beth. Your sister, Beth. She stole the money."

"I don't believe you."

"It's true! Shit, just... shut the door, will you?"

Anna stared at Waldo, her grip on his wrist loosening slightly. Beth? Her sister? The thought seemed absurd, impossible even. But as she looked into Waldo's panicked eyes, she saw a glimmer of truth.

"Tell me everything," Anna demanded, her voice low and dangerous. She wanted to believe that this was all some elaborate lie, but deep down, a part of her feared that Waldo was telling the truth.

Anna reluctantly closed the door, her grip on Waldo's wrist loosening slightly. She took a moment to process the bombshell. Her sister, Beth, had taken the money? It seemed impossible. Her husband Tom was the accountant... Beth was straight-laced. She always had been.

"Where is she?" Anna demanded, her voice sharp with anger and concern.

Waldo hesitated for a moment, seemingly weighing his options. "I... I don't know," he finally admitted. "I swear I don't."

"Tell me what's going on. Tell me everything this time. Leave nothing out, or I swear, I'll throw you off the side of this mountain."

He swallowed, staring into her eyes, and seemed to flinch as he saw something there he didn't seem to like. He hesitated, grimaced, and then he began to talk.

Chapter 17

Morning came quickly, and it saw Waldo Strange the Third tied to a kitchen chair in the small, dank motel Casper had paid for.

Anna drank her second cup of coffee, wiping the sleep from her eyes. She had always managed to get good rest, even in the most trying of situations. It had been one of the many traits she'd picked up while roughing it in the service. Now, though, the scent of coffee helped to heighten her senses as she frowned at Waldo.

"Is this really necessary?" the thief said, shifting back and forth and grimacing as he wiggled in the wooden chair. "I won't run."

"That's what you said last night."

"I didn't!" he pointed out.

"Because Casper caught you and choked you out."

"Right..." he swallowed reflexively, wincing as he did.

Anna could still hear Casper snoring in the other room. If there was one skill the former SEAL had carried over flawlessly, it was the ability to sleep whenever and wherever on demand. Anna supposed she should take the snoring as a compliment and show of the faith he had in her to keep Waldo secured overnight. Ignoring the Casper's buzzsaw sounds, she focused instead on Waldo.

"So tell me again how you heard about this?"

"I told you last night," he said, his voice strained. "You think I'm gonna change my story or something?"

"Humor me."

He sighed, closing his eyes briefly and releasing a long, pent-up breath.

"She didn't know what she was getting in too," he muttered.

"It was a grift."

"A grift. A con. Call it what you want."

"A grift," she repeated.

"Fine. Yes."

"And so you used my sister to rob a crime organization?" Anna said softly, the anger bubbling under the surface of her voice.

"I didn't mean too!" he exclaimed. "I swear. Like I told you, this wasn't my idea. I was out. That weirdo gave me the creeps, so I bailed."

"Your partner? This... albino?"

"Yeah. Real creepy dude. He's like a shark."

Anna crossed her arms. "In what way?"

Waldo shifted uncomfortably in the chair as if reliving a haunting memory. "He's got these dead, cold eyes, you know? Like he's constantly calculating, analyzing every move you make. And his smile... it's this twisted grin that sends shivers down your spine. I didn't trust him from the moment I met him."

"So this guy scared you?"

"I wouldn't say that," Waldo sniffed, trying to maintain some decorum. It was difficult given the ropes binding him to the chair.

"He... he just has this way about him," Waldo stammered, his voice filled with unease. "You know how sharks can sense fear and weakness? Well, he's got that same instinct. It's like he can smell it on you. And once he knows you're vulnerable, he strikes."

Anna leaned in closer, her eyes narrowing as she studied Waldo's face. She could sense the genuine fear emanating from him.

"Tell me about this grift," she demanded, her voice low and commanding.

Waldo took a deep breath, visibly steeling himself before continuing. "So, I knew Beth from way back. We used to run in the same circles, you know? Anyway, we bumped into each other at a bar one night and started talking. Nothing came of it. You know, married and all that."

"You were hitting on her?"

"Yeah, kinda..." Waldo shrugged.

"You really are a sleazebag, aren't you?"

"Sticks and stones, lady."

"Won't break your bones? I know something that might," she said, stepping closer.

He grimaced and quickly said, "Well... okay... so I may have borrowed her wallet when she shot me down."

"Go on," Anna said, a growl to her voice.

"It wasn't... I wasn't trying to do anything," he said quickly. "Just... you know. I needed to make rent... and... I had this meeting later that night and needed bus fare."

"How does any of this drag Beth into stealing eight million dollars?" Anna said testily.

Waldo paused, cleared his throat hesitantly, and glanced sidelong at her. "My wrists really hurt. Mind loosening these ropes a bit?"

"Waldo, spit it out."

"No... I know. I will... just... really, my wrists are—"

"Waldo!"

"Fine!" he exclaimed. He sighed, leaning back, his shaggy hair flopping back and his lean features stretching into a concerned look directed at the ceiling.

She guessed his concern was on his own behalf.

He said, slowly, "I... I had a meeting later that night. And I had her wallet with me."

"My sister's wallet."

"Yeah... that's what I said."

"I'm just clarifying so I don't feel so bad when I knock your teeth in."

"Right," he said hurriedly. "Look... it wasn't ideal. But I told you, this partner of mine, he was a real creep."

"The albino shark."

"Right. Anyway, I wanted out, but he said there was no getting out."

"And?"

"Aaand..." He trailed off. "He asked for the name of someone who could take my place. Said I wasn't going to leave alive unless I gave him a name."

"And?" she repeated, more firmly. She was scowling now. She had a strong suspicion she knew where this was going, and she didn't like it.

"And," he said, "I panicked. Okay. I didn't think it mattered. I... Beth had mentioned that her husband was in accounting. They needed a numbers guy."

"So you gave them Beth's name?" Anna felt her veins go cold. As the pieces of Waldo's story fell together, she didn't feel anger. She was well past that. This conman and thief had just admitted to giving up her sister's family as a scapegoat to save his own skin.

He might not have been thinking about it at the time, but he'd put two innocent children and Anna's sister, her brother-in-law, all of them, on a chopping block to save his own neck.

That cold in Anna's veins very nearly had her reaching for her knife, but instead, she took a long breath, her eyes closed, as she suppressed the urge. She needed him still, and as richly as he might deserve it, Waldo Strange couldn't make it right if he was dead.

"Yeah," he said, wincing. "I didn't think anything of it. I convinced the albino what was what, and I got out of there."

Anna leaned back now, crossing her arms. "So why were you at Beth's place the night her house was burnt to the ground."

"I wasn't," he retorted. "I was there in the morning. Well after the fire started. I heard about it on a scanner and came running."

"Because of the eight million?"

He shrugged. "Like I said, I knew Beth from way back. I felt guilty," he said quickly. "Really. I swear. I never should've given her name."

Anna didn't react at first.

That cold violence in her was still simmering, and the more he talked, the more pitiful he sounded. Now, she just wanted to clock him. But she remained still. For a moment, all she heard was Waldo's heavy breathing as he winced and waited for her reaction.

She could also hear the sound of Casper's intermittent snoring wafting in from the bedroom down the short hall of the cheap motel.

She studied Waldo, reading him as best she could. He was so full of shit, she wasn't sure what was a lie and what was true. He was clearly used to saying whatever it took to save his own hide. His own story had just conceded this point.

"So you're saying they went after my sister... because you gave her name to them?"

"Yeah!"

"So why do they think she has eight million dollars?"

"How's that?"

"Why," she said quietly, "do they think that she has eight million. And how is Los Hermanos involved."

"Los Hermanos were the muscle," Waldo said quickly. "Private contractors. That's all. They had a cop or two in their pocket, you know. So they were useful muscle."

"You sure know a hell of a lot about this scam for someone who walked away."

"I knew the outline," he said. "The broad concept."

"How'd you get in touch with this guy. This albino?"

"Umm... a mutual friend. I did some time a few years ago," he said, shrugging sheepishly. "Made a good impression on my cellmate."

"You really do get around, don't you?"

"A man's gotta eat."

"And so this cellmate put you in contact with the albino. The albino works for a criminal organization that contracted Los Hermanos as muscle... Los Hermanos had cops on the payroll... which was why I found an undercover officer's car at my sister's home after it was burnt..."

She scowled at him again. "And you are the one who gave my sister's name to these killers." She shook her head. "But that doesn't explain why a man calling himself John showed up and told me to return the eight million, Waldo. He seemed to think Beth had it. But why would he think that if Beth was already in his custody?"

Waldo shook his head. "I swear... I don't know. I just... I just know what I've told you."

"Don't swear," she said, shaking her head. "I don't believe you, and it just pisses me off. So when we first spoke... you mentioned none of this."

"I didn't want you to bash my face in!" he exclaimed. "It was an innocent mistake. I just... I had her ID on me because I took her wallet. And when the albino threatened me, I just... handed it to him. Told him she had a special set of skills. Everything he needed. I don't know what happened after that."

"And he just believed you, like that?"

"I can be pretty damn convincing when I need to be."

"Like now?" she pressed, eyes narrowed.

"I'm telling you the truth."

"So you're just a leech... an opportunistic little weasel?"

"I like to think of myself as a businessman," Waldo said, gulping.

She pointed at him, her expression cold. "You put my sister in harm's way. You expect me to believe you just so happened to meet up with her in a bar. You hit on her, then out of revenge when she turned you down, you stole her wallet?"

"That's what happened," he insisted. "Believe it or not, I get around."

"And so... what? They would've looked into Beth. They would've known you were lying."

"I don't know what happened. Maybe they thought she was using her husband's job as cover. I don't know."

"But you were willing to pick through the ruins of her house to find that money, weren't you?" She could feel her blood boiling now. She found her hand clenching into a fist, and she wanted nothing more than to drive it through Waldo's face.

He was grimacing, shaking his head, and stammering, but she was beginning to lose her patience. Nothing he said would make it better. Nothing he said would bring her sister's family back to safety.

She still wasn't even sure she believed any of it. Waldo was the sort of man who spoke in half-truths. He was a liar and a thief. She'd witnessed him picking through the wreckage of her sister's home to steal jewelry. And later that same day, she'd watched him burgle a meth lab. He was not a reliable person, but he was clearly the sort that someone planning a heist might want to recruit.

Was that what had happened?

Waldo had gotten cold feet, and then out of sheer, dumb, bad luck, he'd pushed her sister under the bus?

Maybe it was true... But maybe not.

She needed to know more.

And John, the in-between man who she'd attacked back at the biker's club—he'd said that they had Beth. She'd heard Tom's voice on the phone.

John represented someone who claimed Beth had the eight million.

So what was she missing...

She frowned, shifting back and forth.

And then it suddenly struck her.

"You have the money," she said.

"Wh-what?"

"You have the money," she said more firmly. "But..." she trailed off. "You can't access it. You were at my sister's place looking for... for what? A key? A flashdrive? What were you there for?"

"I don't know what you're talking—"

She punched him. He yelped, tottering in his chair where he was bound. She shoved him in the chest, sending him toppling to the motel kitchen's floor.

As Waldo groaned on the floor, she stood over him, her fists clenched at her sides.

"Tell me the truth!" she seethed, her voice laced with venom. She reached up, brushing her streak of white hair behind her ear.

Waldo groaned again and tried to push himself up. His face was bruised from the punch, blood trickling from his split lip. "I swear, I don't know where the money is!" he pleaded, fear evident in his eyes.

She glared down at him, not buying his act for a second. "You expect me to believe that? You knew about the eight million dollars from the beginning, didn't you? You knew what Los Hermanos wanted, but you couldn't resist the temptation. You completed the job without your partner. You weren't going to turn your nose up at eight million. And then you threw Beth under the bus somehow. You told your partner that she'd taken it... you can be convincing. Is that right? I'm right, aren't I?"

He was starting to shake his head, but her anger kindled. She snatched a knife off the kitchen counter, pointing it at him. "Don't," she snarled.

Waldo's eyes darted around the room, searching for an escape route. Seeing none, he stared at the blade of the knife and swallowed. "What's it with you and sharp instruments?" he said. But he yelped as the knife came closer. "Okay!" he yelled. "Okay, fine... fine... I... I completed the job. Are you happy?"

She stared at him. "Eight million? So why are you robbing meth-heads."

"Because," he snapped, and for the first time, he seemed genuinely upset. "I can't access it. It's in crypto, alright! I have the drive—it has the funds, but I don't have the keycard."

Anna just stared.

"Tom," she said slowly. "Tom works for a financial company. They trade assets. You needed Tom's work info... that's why you were at their house. That's why Beth's name was involved. Not because they stole anything, but because you wanted to use their access. You threw Beth under the bus... That's why they think she's involved. But it's you. You stole the money."

He looked ready to deny it more, but she had heard enough.

It was all starting to click.

Waldo had double-crossed his partner, this albino fellow. He'd blamed Beth. Perhaps claiming she was an insider who could unlock the crypto flashdrive he'd stolen.

"They got to her first," Waldo said suddenly, his voice strained. "I swear... I was going to cut her in. Two million, but she refused."

Anna stared at him.

"Who turns down two million?" Waldo moaned.

"They traced my phone calls to Beth. They probably thought she was my partner."

"I don't even know what to believe when you talk," Anna snapped.

"I know... I know," Waldo said. "But my phone! My phone, you can check the voicemail she left me. Beth left me a voicemail!" he said urgently. "She turned down my offer. Insane, right?"

"Beth wouldn't be bribed. Neither would Tom," Anna said with a snarl. "Where's your damn phone?" She reached into his pocket and yanked out his device, her anger fueling her every action. She snatched his finger, and he yelped as she twisted it behind his back to press the biometric scanner. She quickly navigated through his voicemail, searching for the message that Waldo claimed Beth had left him.

As she listened to the message, her heart sank. It was Beth's voice, filled with fear and desperation. Beth was saying, "I received your message, Mr. Cartwright..." Waldo winced at the mention of another alias, ducking his head sheepishly. "But I simply can't accept," Beth said. "I'm going to the police tomorrow. Please don't call me or my husband again."

The line went dead.

Anna repeated it, listening to her sister's voice and feeling that cold, lethal anger rising again.

She tossed the phone back at Waldo.

"Wait!" he pleaded, his voice trembling. "I can help you find them, I swear!"

"Where's the eight million?" Anna said suddenly. "Give it to me. I'll trade it for them."

Waldo paused. "I... It's not going to work. They're going to kill her anyway," he said.

"Where's the money," she snarled.

Waldo went ashen-faced, tight-lipped. "I don't have it on me."

"Where is it?" she repeated. "I'm not going to ask again."

Chapter 18

Waldo sat in the back seat, his hands bound and his mouth gagged.

The gag had been Anna's idea. Casper sat in the passenger seat, while Anna was driving; she kept glancing in the rearview mirror as they moved down the old, dusty roads.

Anna was glaring at Waldo, her eyes narrowed. "If you're lying," she said, her voice low and cold, "I'm going to drop you off where I found you. Those meth dealers will be more than excited to see you again, I'm sure."

Waldo just shook his head adamantly, trying to speak, but his voice was muffled by the gag.

The sun dipped low in the sky, casting long shadows across the cracked asphalt of the old road. Dust swirled up around the tires of the unassuming sedan, obscuring its faded maroon paint job as it sped down the narrow path. Inside the car, a thick air of tension weighed heavy on the three occupants.

Anna gripped the steering wheel with white knuckles as she navigated the potholes and overgrown edges. Her mind raced with thoughts of what might be waiting for them at their destination. Casper sat in the passenger seat, his eyes darting between Anna and the bound figure in the backseat.

"Are you sure this is the right way?" Casper asked, breaking the silence that had stretched between them.

"Positive," Anna replied, her voice tight and controlled. "This is the most direct route to the docks."

Waldo's muffled protests from the backseat added an unnerving soundtrack to their journey. The stark contrast between the serenity of the surrounding countryside and the urgency of their mission gnawed at Anna's nerves.

"Alright, enough," she said, glancing in the rearview mirror at their captive. Pulling off onto the shoulder, she shifted the car into park and turned to face Waldo.

Anna leaned into the backseat, her left hand deftly removing the gag from Waldo's mouth while her right remained poised near her concealed weapon. She could feel the sweat bead on her brow as she stared into Waldo's fearful eyes.

"Tell me exactly where the hidden USB drive is on the yacht," she demanded, her voice low and menacing.

Waldo swallowed hard, beads of perspiration dotting his forehead as he met Anna's unwavering gaze. "I-it's in the captain's quarters," he stammered, his voice raspy from disuse. "There's a secret compartment behind the mirror on the wall. You need to press the lower right corner and it'll pop open."

"Is it guarded?" Casper interjected, his brow furrowed with concern.

"Two guys, maybe three," Waldo replied, his voice growing steadier. "But they don't know about the compartment. They're just there to keep intruders off the yacht. An old client of mine showed me the hidey-hole. He's in prison. It's fine. Now, really... is the gag necessary?"

Anna ignored this last comment and processed the information, her mind calculating potential scenarios and outcomes. If Waldo was telling the truth, she could handle two or three guards - but if he was leading them into a trap, things could quickly spiral out of control. Her pulse quickened at the thought, but she kept her emotions in check, her face betraying no uncertainty.

"Alright," she said, nodding curtly. "We'll be there soon. Make sure you're telling the truth, because if you're not, I promise you'll regret it."

GUARDIAN'S VENGEANCE

Without another word, Anna replaced Waldo's gag, despite his muffled protests. She exchanged a quick glance with Casper before stepping out of the car and surveying the private dock ahead of them. The sun was still cresting the sky, introducing the morning.

"Stay here with Waldo," she instructed Casper, her voice barely audible above the hum of the car's engine. "I'll be back as soon as I have the USB drive."

Casper nodded. "Be careful," he murmured.

Anna inhaled deeply, feeling the cool morning air fill her lungs as she mentally prepared herself for the task at hand. Her training kicked in, allowing her to push away any lingering doubts or fears. She was no stranger to high-stakes situations, and this was just another mission - one she couldn't afford to fail.

Silently, she approached the water's edge, her keen eyes scanning the area for any potential obstacles. The security gate loomed ahead, a formidable barrier between her and the yacht that held the key to her family's safety.

A few early-morning boaters were gathered near the keypad at the gate. A single guard was stationed, greeting a couple of older gentlemen with a friendly wave. None of them had spotted her yet.

She moved around the side of the dock, keeping her distance from the main gate.

Once she was hidden behind a particularly large bait shack, standing in the shadows, she moved toward the water.

Her boots hit the surf with a gentle splash, the cold liquid sending a shiver up her spine. Despite the chill, Anna remained focused, her thoughts centered on the task at hand. Swiftly, she submerged herself in the murky depths, her years of experience guiding her movements as she swam toward the fence encircling the moored boats.

The icy tendrils of the water seemed to wrap themselves around her limbs, threatening to slow her down, but Anna refused to let anything hinder her progress. She could feel the pressure building in her ears as she drew closer to the fence, knowing that every second counted.

With a final burst of strength, she propelled herself under the fence, her body gliding through the narrow space like a fish. Emerging on the other side, she took a moment to catch her breath, grateful for the cover of the dock's shadow that cloaked her movements.

Anna clung to the edge of the dock, muscles tense and eyes darting across the deck of the yacht. Sunlight glinted off the metal railings, casting eerie shadows that seemed to dance in time with the gently lapping waves. She scanned for any signs of movement, her breaths shallow and controlled as she tried to remain undetected.

"Patience," Anna reminded herself, trying to silence the voice in her head that whispered about the ticking clock.

Two men were moving about on deck, wearing dark suits, and looking bored.

The private security for the boat... She cataloged their movements, committing them to memory as if it were some sort of dance.

Finally, spotting a break in the guards' patrol, Anna heaved herself out of the water and onto the dock. Deftly, she switched her handgun to her left hand, feeling a sense of comfort in the weapon's familiar weight. Her heart raced as she crept up the gangway, each step calculated to avoid detection.

"Alright, Waldo," she muttered under her breath, her thoughts returning to their captive. "You better not be playing games."

The room where Waldo claimed the USB drive was hidden lay just down the hall from the main deck. As she approached, Anna could hear the low murmur of voices and laughter echoing through the corridors. Her instincts screamed at her to be cautious; trusting Waldo was a gamble.

She slipped into the room, relieved to find it empty, her gaze immediately drawn to the intricate wooden paneling that lined the walls. A mirror was stationed above an old couch. According to Waldo, the drive was concealed behind one of the mirror's multiple panels.

She approached a mirror. Carefully, Anna crouched down and began to search, her fingers tracing the ornate carvings in search of a hidden latch or seam.

"Come on," she whispered, frustration creeping into her voice as precious seconds ticked by. "Where are you?"

Her pulse pounded in her ears, drowning out the distant sounds of revelry from elsewhere on the yacht. It was a race against time, and Anna knew she couldn't afford any mistakes. She had to find the drive, secure the crypto, and get back to Casper before their window of opportunity closed. Once she had the flashdrive with the eight million, she'd have leverage to get her family back. Unless of course, Waldo was somehow selling *her* out too, maybe to clear some of the bad blood with his albino associate.

Anna shook her head, clearing the distracting thought. She chided herself, pushing aside the nagging suspicion that Waldo had led her into a trap. Now was not the time.

As her fingers finally found purchase on a small, hidden switch, Anna felt a surge of triumph. The panel swung open, revealing the USB drive nestled within a concealed compartment.

"Gotcha," she breathed, snatching the drive and pocketing it. She allowed herself a brief moment of satisfaction before the gravity of the situation came crashing back down. There was no time to waste; she needed to get off the yacht and back to Casper before they were discovered.

Just then, her phone buzzed.

She frowned, glancing down.

It was Casper.

She hesitated but decided that her old military buddy wouldn't be calling unless it was crucial.

She answered the phone, lingering in the shadows. "Casper?" she said.

"I had a chat with the asshole," Casper replied.

"Oh?"

"He only gave you half a truth."

"What's that?"

Casper grunted, "He got talkative."

"What did you do to make him talkative?" Anna asked.

"They don't call me the Friendly Ghost for nothing," Casper quipped back. "Probably likes me better because I don't tie him to chairs and threaten to stab him. People are funny that way."

"Casper—"

"You know, these are the sorts of people skills you pick up when you *stop* thinking of other people in terms of how you'd kill them and *start* accepting people's offers of French fries and—"

"Casper!" Anna kept her voice nearly silent, but the edge in it was unmistakable.

"Ok, ok," Casper said, his voice carrying that same conversational aloofness as everything else he said. "Waldo says the flashdrive is in two parts. One behind the mirror and the other under floor paneling in the bedroom adjacent to that room. Under the bed."

Anna frowned. "He failed to mention that earlier."

"Yeh, well... Like I said, I'm a people person." In the background, Anna could hear Waldo inarticulately whining. "You're fine!" Casper said, his voice turned away from the phone mic before returning to Anna. "Big baby. I may have given him a couple love taps during our heart to heart. He's got raccoon eyes now."

Anna pictured two black eyes framing Waldo's face, and she didn't feel much in the way of pity.

"So you think he's telling the truth?"

"Yeah, isn't that right, Mr. Strange?"

She heard a muttered response in the background, but then Casper said, "You'll wanna find an old wooden door. Back of the room with the mirror."

A faint moaning sound from a nearby room caught Anna's attention, making her grimace. She wasn't alone. She slowly lowered the phone and focused on her surroundings.

The first drive secured in her pocket, she carefully approached the door from which the sounds emanated.

Her eyes darted around the hall to ensure no one was approaching. Her left hand, steady as ever, rested lightly on her holstered gun, ready to react if necessary.

Steeling her nerves, Anna cracked open the door, wincing at the soft creak it emitted. Peering inside, her eyes widened at the sight before her: a rotund man lay sprawled across a bed, his flabby mass quivering with each deep moan that escaped his lips. A muscular masseuse, sweat glistening on his biceps, worked his large hands over the fat man's back, kneading the flesh beneath his fingers.

For a brief moment, she considered retreating and making her way back to Casper, but she'd come too far to back out now. She'd dealt with unreliable witnesses and information sources before. Waldo was no exception. Sometimes, it was like pulling teeth. But she had one USB drive in hand, exactly where he'd said it would be. And she trusted Casper's instincts. If he'd extracted the location of a second device, then he was likely onto something.

With a silent sigh, she slipped into the room, pressing her back against the wall to avoid detection. She watched as the masseuse's hands moved with surprising grace over the man's mountainous form.

The fat man grunted between moans, his eyes locked on the ceiling. "You're good."

"Thank you, sir," the masseuse replied with a curt nod, his voice devoid of any warmth.

As Anna observed the scene, she felt a growing sense of unease. The second partition of the USB drive was under the bed. She found herself frowning now. How was she supposed to get there without being seen?

The large, muscular masseuse' back was to her. He wasn't wearing a shirt, and his muscles strained against his dark skin. The other man was still staring at the ceiling.

The heavy scent of sweat and massage oil hung in the air, making Anna's nostrils flare with distaste. As she lingered in the shadows, her eyes darted back and forth between the fat man and his muscular masseuse. She weighed her options, knowing that time was slipping away from her.

She tried to ease around the side of the room, but as she moved, the floor creaked.

The fat man on the bed looked up suddenly, his eyes alert like a hawk's.

He stared right at her.

She stared back, hand tensed on her weapon.

"Oi! Who are you?" The fat man's voice cut through the room, his tone dripping with suspicion as his gaze locked onto Anna. The masseuse's hands ceased their rhythmic motion, and he turned sharply, his ice-blue eyes narrowing dangerously.

"Wrong room," Anna replied tersely, attempting to back out the door.

"Wait!" The fat man's voice halted her retreat. "Do I know you?"

"Can't say you do," Anna said, taking a deep breath. She could feel the weight of the USB drive pressing against her pocket, a reminder of the stakes at hand. She'd have to come back later for the second drive. "Now, if you'll excuse me—"

"Don't let her leave!" the rotund fellow barked.

The masseuse's muscles rippled.

He lunged towards her, his face twisted into a snarl. "You're not going anywhere!"

Anna's instincts kicked in. With swift, calculated movements, she ducked under the giant's outstretched arm and aimed an elbow strike at his solar plexus, forcing the wind from his lungs.

"Ugh!" The giant doubled over, gasping for breath. Anna didn't hesitate, bringing her knee up into his face with a sickening crunch. Blood sprayed across the room, and the giant crumpled to the floor.

"Holy shit!" The fat man scrambled backward on the bed, terror etched in every crease of his face. "Who are you?"

"Someone who doesn't have time for this," Anna snapped, her heart racing as adrenaline coursed through her veins. She knew she couldn't afford to linger any longer; someone would have heard the commotion. "Stay out of my way."

With that, she rushed at the bed, dropping to the ground, and peering in the space under the overburdened piece of furniture.

The man on the bed yelped as she came near, but she had no interest in him.

Instead, she was scanning the floorboards under the bed, moving desperately.

The masseuse was groaning behind her, clutching his face. Ignoring this, Anna quickly located the loose floorboard. With a swift motion, she pried it open and found a small compartment hidden beneath. Her eyes widened as she saw the second USB drive nestled inside. Grabbing it, she wasted no time in slipping it into her pocket next to the first drive.

"Hey, stop! Stop!" Squawked the man on the bed, but she was quite done with following unsolicited directions. Her pulse raced with every silent footfall as she retraced her steps to where she had slipped past security.

Before she submerged, she pulled the double plastic bags she'd been provided by Casper. She wrapped both flash drives, bound them tightly, and slipped them back into her pocket.

The murky water of the private dock shimmered, reflecting the sunlight that guided her path. With a deep breath and one last glance around the yacht, Anna eased herself back into the water.

Her muscles tensed against the cold, but she pushed through it, focusing on the SEAL training that had become instinct. She skillfully maneuvered under the fence encircling the moored boats, her movements fluid and precise. Once she cleared the perimeter, Anna swam toward Casper's car, waiting just beyond the dock.

"Did you get it?" Casper's voice was laced with curiosity as he opened the car door and threw a towel in Anna's direction.

"Got it right here," she replied, wrapping the towel around her freezing body and tapping the USB drives in her pocket. "Now let's get the hell out of here."

Waldo was still in the back seat, and he looked miserable. Gagged, bound, and now sporting two black eyes and a bloody nose, he kept glaring sullenly at them.

Anna just gave him a once over, then snorted.

Casper nodded and accelerated away from the dock, tires kicking up dust as they sped down the old road.

"Anna, are you alright?" Casper asked, casting a glance in her direction.

"Fine, just... someone messaged me," she muttered as her phone buzzed. Picking it up, she read the text from "John" aloud.

"Rendezvous location confirmed. GPS link attached. Your family is in danger. You have twenty-four hours."

She stared at the message. The number was unknown, but John had signed it with his name at the top. She briefly wondered what the mysterious liaison's real name was but knew she was unlikely to ever know. Instead, her mind focused on the more pressing matter—

The time limit.

Anna stared at the threatening message. "Damn it!" Anna slammed her fist against the dashboard.

Casper didn't say anything but kept his eyes on the road.

She paused, inhaling slowly, and trying to calm herself. Waldo looked miserable in the back seat, but she shot him an angry glance. If not for him, and his meddling, her sister wouldn't be in this mess.

She tapped her fingers against the dashboard, trying to let the tactile response refocus her.

Anna clenched her fists, knuckles turning white as she tried to suppress the overwhelming fury and fear threatening to consume her. Her eyes darted between the road ahead and the USB drives now held in her palm, a cold reminder of the stakes involved. The text message from "John" burned in her mind like an itch she couldn't scratch. Every second that passed put her family in greater danger, and she knew she had to find a solution.

"We have the money now," she rattled off. "We have leverage."

"But we don't have the key," said Casper, glancing at her. He jutted a finger towards Waldo in the back seat. "This asshole doesn't have access to the money."

"But Tom does."

"Beth's husband, right?"

"Yeah. He works on this stuff. They stole the safe, but not the key to the lock."

"So Waldo here had the safe, and this... what did you call him, albino guy? He has the key in Tom."

"Exactly."

Casper shook his head. "What's to stop them from putting a bullet in your brother-in-law's head the moment they get what they want?"

"Nothing," Anna said with a growl, "but do you have a better idea?"

Just then, the phone began to ring.

She stared. It was the same unknown number that had just texted her. John was trying to call. Anna felt a shudder down her spine, and she scowled at the screen. For a moment, she half wanted to fling the device across the car and shatter it. But cooler heads prevailed; she shared a look with Casper, then answered the call from her sister's kidnapper.

Chapter 19

"Hello?" Anna's voice was laced with tension and suspicion as she held the phone to her ear.

"Anna," a deep, gravelly voice greeted her. "I trust you received my message."

"Who is this?" Anna demanded, her grip on the steering wheel tightening.

"John," the voice said.

"You're not the guy I talked with back at the bar," she snapped. "He was a sniveling weasel. Who are you?"

The voice chuckled. "John. And like my colleague, John, I represent the same interests."

"You're not Los Hermanos," she said.

"We work with many contractors. But this isn't about us," the new John said on the phone. "I need to ensure that you're willing to cooperate."

"I'm not playing games with you," Anna snapped, a trace of anger seeping into her voice. "If you harm my family—"

"Ah, ah, ah," John interrupted, a sinister chuckle emanating from the other end of the line. "Threats won't get you anywhere. I assure you, your loved ones are safe for now. But if you want them to remain that way, you'll do exactly as I say."

Anna felt a surge of frustration and helplessness wash over her. She couldn't let her emotions cloud her judgment; she needed to focus on finding a way out of this predicament.

"What do I need to do?" she asked through gritted teeth, trying to keep her voice steady.

"There's a small abandoned industrial complex on the outskirts of Mammoth Lakes," John instructed. "Come alone and bring the money with you. We'll exchange it for your family."

"And how do I know they'll be released once I hand over the funds?" Anna pressed, her brows furrowing in skepticism.

"You have no choice. You have what we want. And we have what you want. Come alone, or your family pays the price."

Anna's heart pounded in her chest as she processed the ultimatum. She glanced at Casper, who met her gaze with a mixture of concern and suspicion. There was no way she could go alone. It was too risky.

"I'm coming," Anna said firmly into the phone, her voice devoid of any fear.

"What? You're not serious, right?" Casper whispered, his eyes widening in disbelief.

Anna held up a hand to silence him before returning her attention to the call. "I'll be there, but I won't come alone. I have someone with me who knows where the money is."

There was a moment of silence on the other end before the voice responded, "Fine. Bring them, but remember, any tricks and your family pays."

With that, the line went dead. Anna let out a breath she hadn't realized she was holding and looked over at Casper.

"We need a plan," he stated, his voice not quite as aloof as it had been before.

Anna nodded in agreement. "How do you feel about another favor?"

"You still owe me for the last one."

Right. Anna had promised to let Casper in on why she was discharged. Letting out a stiff snort, Anna shook her head, speaking in a low, resigned voice.

"I punched out a SEAL commander," she said softly. "And that was only the start. It's not even the main course of what happened. You want the full story? I'll give it. I just need some help, Casper." She looked at her old partner-in-crime.

He sighed and then nodded once.

"Deal. I'm a sucker for a cliffhanger."

Chapter 20

Beth's heart pounded in her chest as she gripped the cold metal pipe tightly. Sweat coated her palms, but she couldn't afford to let it slip. She could picture her children, Tony and Sarah, huddled together behind the door, on the other side of the room, their eyes wide with fear and confusion. The eerie silence of the room wrapped around them like a suffocating shroud.

"Stand back," Beth whispered hoarsely, unable to tear her gaze from the locked wooden door that stood between her and her offspring. "Stay back, dears. Please. Are you away from the door?"

A pause, then Tony's small voice. "Yes."

Beth took a deep breath, steeling herself for what was about to come. With every ounce of strength she could muster, she raised the pipe high above her head and slammed it into the door.

The sound reverberated through the room, shaking her to the core. She could hear her pulse roaring in her ears, drowning out everything else.

The door trembled under the force of her blow, but the lock remained stubbornly intact. Desperation clawed at her insides, threatening to consume her. She had to get through; she had to protect her children from whatever awaited them on the other side. But the more she tried to suppress it, the louder the whisper of doubt grew in the recesses of her mind. What if she couldn't break through? What if they were trapped here?

"Mom..." Sarah's voice quivered from the dark, muffled by the door.

"Stay quiet, sweetheart," Beth said, choking back her own tears. She couldn't let her resolve crumble now – not when her children needed her the most. She steadied herself, ignoring the throbbing pain in her arms, and swung the pipe against the door once more.

The door groaned, and the sound of splintering wood echoed through the silence. The lock was starting to give way, but it wasn't enough. Not yet. With a silent prayer, Beth adjusted her grip on the pipe and prepared for another strike.

"Be ready," she whispered to Tony and Sarah.

She swung the pipe again, feeling the impact reverberate through her body. The door shuddered, and the lock began to give way. Almost there.

"Mom, I'm scared," Sarah whimpered.

"Me too, kiddo," Beth admitted quietly, more to herself than to her daughter. She couldn't let fear rule her now. Not when so much was at stake. She took a deep breath, trying to steady her trembling hands. "But we're going to be okay. I promise."

Her children had gone silent now.

She hesitated. They were no longer sobbing. In fact, she couldn't hear their panicked breaths anymore.

Was her mind simply playing tricks?

"Tony?" she called out. "Sarah?"

No response.

She tried a bit louder, her voice hoarse. "Tony? Sarah?"

Still no reply.

A cold, creeping dread crept down her spine.

With a final surge of strength, she swung the pipe at the lock, feeling it crack beneath the force of the blow. The door swung open with an abruptness that caught her off guard, and for a moment, all she could do was stare at the darkness that lay beyond.

Beth stumbled into the dimly lit room, her heart thundering in her chest as her eyes struggled to adjust to the shadows. Her breath hitched when she discerned the unexpected sight of her children standing beside a pale-haired man. The contrast between their petite forms and his tall, imposing figure sent a shiver down her spine.

"Mom?" Sarah's voice wavered, her wide blue eyes filled with confusion and fear as she stared at Beth.

Beth went still, absolute terror curdling her soul. She stared at the familiar man, their kidnapper.

"Quiet, child," the man commanded, his voice smooth and deep, like poisoned honey. The albino, dressed in a neat, tailored suit, stroked Sarah's blonde hair with a tenderness that felt unsettling amidst the tense situation. He turned to face Beth, his eerie red eyes locking onto hers.

"Get your hands off my daughter," Beth snarled, her maternal rage overpowering the terror that threatened to consume her.

Every instinct told her to grab her children and run, but there was nowhere to run. The man had clearly come down the stairwell visible in the back of the room. And he wasn't alone. Two large men stood at the base of the stairwell, watching the scene with cold calculation.

What did he want, and why had he chosen to involve her children?

"Be honest, Beth," the man said as if reading her thoughts. "You need my help..." he continued stroking her daughter's hair. "And I need yours."

"Help with what?" Beth asked, her voice shaking.

"First, let me assure your children's safety," he said, his eyes never leaving hers. "At least... for now."

He stepped forward now, his hand lowering from Sarah's hair. He faced Beth, his gaze cold and calculating.

The two gunmen flanked the man like statues, their expressions and unwavering gazes amplifying the dread that gripped Beth's heart. The weapons in their hands were a stark reminder of the danger they posed, and their mere presence heightened her sense of urgency. She clenched her fists, nails digging into her palms, as she tried to maintain an outward appearance of strength.

"Tell me, Beth," the man said, his voice smooth but chilling, "do you love your children?"

His icy gaze pierced through her, and Beth felt a shudder run down her spine. The question, so simple and innocent, was laden with terrifying implications. She swallowed hard, trying to summon her courage before responding.

"Of course I do," she said, her voice barely more than a whisper. The answer wasn't for him but for them. "More than anything."

"Then," he continued, his calm demeanor never faltering, "you should be willing to go to any lengths to protect them, shouldn't you?"

Beth's eyes darted from the pale-haired man to the gunmen and back again, her mind racing with the possible outcomes this conversation could have. She thought of Tony and Sarah huddled together, their fear palpable. They were depending on her now more than ever.

"Whatever it is that you want," she began, her voice shaking slightly, "please, leave my children out of this."

"Your concern for your offspring is admirable," the man replied, his tone unreadable. "But your cooperation will determine their safety."

"Please," she pleaded, her desperation threatening to overwhelm her. "I don't know what you're after, but let them go. They're innocent."

"Indeed," he said, leaning in closer, his eyes never leaving hers. "Their innocence is what makes them such valuable bargaining chips, Beth. So I suggest you think carefully about your next move."

Beth's heart ached as she looked into the man's cold, unfeeling eyes. She felt her chest tighten, her breath hitching as fear clawed at her very core. Her children were so close, yet so far away.

"Please," she sobbed, tears streaming down her cheeks. "Please, let them go. They've done nothing wrong."

"Nothing wrong?" The man echoed, tilting his head with false curiosity. "Perhaps not. But you, on the other hand..."

He leaned in closer, his icy gaze piercing through her. Beth shivered involuntarily, recoiling from the contact. It was as if he could see her every thought, her deepest fears.

"Give me the encryption key for the money, Beth," he demanded, his voice a low growl. "And I'll consider releasing your precious children."

Beth blinked, her mind spinning. What money? What encryption key? She had no idea what he was talking about, but she knew that admitting that would only put her children in more danger.

"Please," she whispered, her voice barely audible. "Just let them go. I beg you."

The man studied her carefully, his expression unreadable.

"Very well," he said finally, his tone flat. "But remember, Beth: actions have consequences. And you're running out of time."

He stepped back, gesturing to the gunmen who had been standing silently beside him. As they moved forward, guns trained on her, Beth tensed.

"Bring her," the pale-haired man ordered, his voice devoid of emotion. "And make sure she understands the stakes."

As the gunmen seized her roughly, Beth's eyes darted to Tony and Sarah one last time. Their faces were etched with fear.

"Mom!" Tony cried out, his voice cracking.

Sarah's eyes filled with tears, her tiny, trembling form shaking like a leaf in the cold, dark room.

The air between them seemed to crackle with tension, and Beth could feel the weight of the pale-haired man's cold gaze as she shook her head, desperately. "No, no, please! I don't know any code," she insisted, her voice shaking. "You have to believe me."

"Is that so?" the albino asked, his anger simmering beneath a thin veil of composure. He took a step closer, leaning down until he was mere inches from Beth's face. She could see the barely restrained fury burning in his red eyes. "Then perhaps you need a little incentive to remember."

"Please," Beth whispered, her chest tightening as panic threatened to overtake her. "I'm telling the truth. I don't know anything about an encryption code or money."

"Enough!" the man exploded, his patience finally snapping. He straightened up, the controlled calm of his demeanor shattered. "You will give me that code, or your children will pay the price!"

Beth's heart raced as she searched his face for any hint of mercy, but there was none to be found. She felt tears welling up in her eyes, but she refused to let them fall. "I can't give you what I don't know," she said, her voice stronger than she thought possible. "Please, just let my children go."

"Every second you waste brings them closer to their end, Mrs. Gabriel. I will not ask again."

Beth clenched her hands into tight fists, the last shreds of hope evaporating as she met the man's icy gaze. "I told you, I don't know any code. I have no idea what encryption key you're talking about!" she insisted, her voice wavering but determined. "You have to believe me."

"Is that so?" He took a step closer, leaning down until he was mere inches from Beth's face. She could see the barely restrained fury burning in his icy pink eyes.

"Please," Beth whispered, her chest tightening as panic threatened to overtake her.

For a moment, they simply stared, his cold eyes meeting hers. The albino clicked his fingers, and the two gunmen who'd approached her snatched her by the wrists. As they dragged her away, Beth's panicked sobs soon drowned out the distant screaming of her children.

Chapter 21

The sun was at its zenith when Anna stirred from her nap, blinking away the remnants of sleep. She glanced over at Casper, who was driving. They'd switched on and off in an effort to reach their destination.

Anna perked up nearly instantly, her senses coming around. Her body was honed to wake quickly; in the field, one didn't have the opportunity to dawdle before coming to their senses. The digital clock on the dashboard read 12:02 PM—she had slept longer than intended.

"Damn, it's already noon," Anna muttered, stretching her left arm behind her head. She could feel a dull ache in her shoulder. Her right hand instinctively clenched and unclenched, remembering the countless times she had pulled a trigger and realizing, though she'd forgotten it, that her dreams had been violent o
nes.

"We there yet?" she shot at Casper.

He grunted, turning down a side street and nodding ahead. "Just up there."

"Didn't realize it was this long of a drive."

"You said you wanted the best. Eduardo is the best." He shot her a look. "You sure you need this much hardware?"

"I'm sure."

Anna scanned their surroundings. They had arrived at a run-down part of the city, where the very air seemed heavy with decay. Buildings on either side were boarded up or crumbling, their facades stained with soot and grime.

As they pulled up to what appeared to be a drive-thru window, the absence of any fast food signs was conspicuous. Instead, rusted bars covered the glass, while graffiti marred the surrounding walls. Anna couldn't help but feel a pang of unease as she surveyed the desolate scene before them.

"Alright, let's get this over with," she said, her voice steady despite the uncertainty churning in her gut. Casper nodded in agreement, his own apprehension masked behind a practiced, stoic expression.

Anna glanced towards the rearview mirror, catching sight of Waldo bound and gagged in the back seat. Her anger flared at his betrayal, but she knew she needed to keep a clear head for what was to come.

He was fidgeting uncomfortably and continued to glance out the window as they slowed near the drive-thru as if looking for a chance to escape.

"Stay put, Waldo" she spat, her voice cold. "You've done enough damage already." The helpless man let out muffled whimpers of protest, his eyes darting between Anna and Casper.

Casper muttered under his breath, shaking his head in disgust. "Let's get our gear and get the hell out of here."

As they inched closer to the drive-thru speaker, an uneasy silence enveloped them. High walls on either side seemed to close in, creating a sense of isolation and secrecy that only heightened their anxiety. An empty billboard loomed above them, its faded and peeling paint hinting at a forgotten promise of something better.

"You'd think they'd at least have some decent signage." Casper mused, trying to break the tension.

"Maybe that's the point," Anna replied, her eyes narrowing as she studied the decrepit speaker box. "Keeps the wrong people from finding it. Plus, it doesn't exactly scream 'black market arms dealer', does it?"

"True," Casper conceded, shifting uncomfortably in his seat.

"You've been here before, right?"

"Yeah. Few times. Looks worse than I remember. Eduardo isn't much one for appearances."

"Just so long as we don't get shot."

"Right," he nodded, taking a deep breath as they pulled to a stop by the old, drive-thru speaker. "Let's do this."

Casper leaned out the window, his nimble fingers tapping away at the screen under the order tablet. The twenty-digit code seemed to stretch on forever, each number meticulously entered with a precision only someone like Casper could manage. With a final tap, the speaker crackled to life.

He sent the text and then reached out the window, hitting a red button.

Then they waited.

Anna and Casper shared a look.

The crackling speaker buzzed with static, the sound echoing through the decrepit surroundings. Anna's heart pounded in her chest as she waited for a response, each passing second feeling like an eternity.

Suddenly, a voice emerged from the speaker, distorted and garbled. "State your business," it demanded, sounding more like a ghostly whisper than a human voice.

Casper leaned closer to the speaker, his voice firm and authoritative. "We're here for the trade," he replied, his tone laced with determination.

There was a brief pause before the voice on the other end replied, "Prove your loyalty."

Anna's grip tightened around the steering wheel as she exchanged another glance with Casper.

He just shook his head. The way the voice spoke, it sounded like he was expecting some sort of response or passcode.

"Brand Loyalty is capitalist dogma," Casper replied, sounding a little like a drive-thru worker himself, his words clearly English but with none of the inflection to indicate they meant anything at all.

Immediately, the voice on the speaker changed from demanding and ominous to something far more energetic and excited.

"Ah, my favorite customer!" boomed the voice through the rusted grates of the drive-thru speaker. "Casper, old friend!"

"Eduardo," Casper replied, leaning back in the driver's seat and staring at the speaker with hooded eyes."

"Surprised you'd come around here again," said Eduardo.

Anna tensed at the edge in the voice.

"Oh?" said Casper. "And why's that?"

"You don't remember?"

"Remember what, Eddie? You're not still sore about the game are you?"

"I'm still not sure how you managed to win that hand. And don't call me Eddie."

"Fine... Tony," Casper replied.

Anna blinked. Tony Eduardo? She'd heard the name before. He had a reputation in the Pacific Northwest for running an underground network of arms dealers. If Casper knew him personally, it meant they were in the right place.

Casper leaned closer to the speaker again, his voice low and conspiratorial. "We need your expertise, Tony. We've got a job coming up, and we require some top-of-the-line hardware."

There was a pause on the other end before Tony's voice crackled through the speaker once more. "Hardware, you say? Well, you've come to the right place. I've got just what you need... just, make sure you have the right count, this time."

A pause.

Casper scowled. "Really? You want to do this now?"

"Now? Don't know what you mean, bud. Just surprised you won that last hand is all."

"Likewise, Tony," Casper replied. "But let's be honest here, we both know you had an ace up your sleeve."

"Me? Cheat?" Tony Eduardo feigned offense, his voice dripping with sarcasm. "Never! I'm as honest as they come!"

Anna rolled her eyes, her patience wearing thin. She cleared her throat loudly, her annoyance evident. "Gentlemen, we're on a bit of a tight schedule here."

"Of course," Tony said, his voice now all business. "You brought a friend with you, Casp? Who's the lovely lady?"

Anna couldn't see the camera, but she knew she was being watched.

"An old friend," Casper replied. "She's trustworthy."

"Your vouch means a thing or two, I guess... Despite the poker hand..."

"Can we get to it, Ed—I mean, Tony."

"My apologies. So, what can I help you two with today?"

"Actually, it's more about what you can provide us with," Casper interjected, his demeanor shifting from annoyed to serious. "We need some specific hardware."

Anna couldn't help but glance at the rearview mirror and catch a glimpse of Waldo, tied up and gagged in the backseat. Perhaps he could prove useful. But now was not the time for that—she needed to focus on securing the weapons first.

"Tony, make sure everything is top-notch," Casper said, his voice firm. "We can't afford any slip-ups."

"Trust me, my friend," Tony replied confidently. "I only deal in the best."

Anna nodded, her mind already racing through the plan. The industrial district was their rendezvous location, and she would need to keep a constant eye out for potential threats. She knew that she would have to neutralize the bad guys before they had a chance to harm her family.

Casper glanced at Anna and nodded toward the speaker as if inviting her to lean in.

She did, clearing her throat. Then, with practiced precision, she rattled off, "First, we'll need a PVS-14 Gen 3 night vision monocular with a helmet mount," she said, her voice confident and precise. "Then, I want a Barrett M82A1 .50 caliber sniper rifle with a Nightforce ATACR F1 scope. Additionally, we'll need a bipod, suppressor, and hard case for transport."

"Sounds like you know your stuff," Tony replied. "I can get all of that for you. Just pull up to the second window."

Anna blinked. "Just like that?"

"Honey, we got everything. Pull on up."

Casper started the car again, and they drove forward to the next window. The smell of grease wafted in through their open windows as they passed by the remnants of what used to be a drive-thru kitchen.

An Italian man with a golden tooth greeted them with a wide grin when they reached the second window. His eyes flickered momentarily to Waldo in the backseat before returning to Anna and Casper. The man was a small, scrawny fellow with spiky, black hair, and enough gold chains around his neck that she suspected he'd sink in a bathtub.

He was scratching at his nose and sniffing every couple of seconds.

"So. You got the cash?"

Anna handed him a folder full of cash, freshly withdrawn from an ATM earlier that day. As the man counted the bills, she couldn't help but study the worn-out buildings surrounding them. Her eye fixated on the best lookout spots.

As Tony Eduardo counted the money, he kept glancing up at Casper.

"What?" Casper said after this happened a third time.

"Oh, nothing, bud," the Italian man said, pausing his counting to look up.

Casper rolled his eyes and sighed. "Tony, we've been over this a dozen times. You lost fair and square. Can we just move on?"

Tony Eduardo chuckled, his eyes glinting mischievously. "You always did have a way with cards, Casper."

After what felt like an eternity of counting, Tony finally nodded in approval. "All accounted for," he declared, slipping the cash into a hidden compartment beneath the counter. "Give me a moment, and I'll bring out your merchandise."

She couldn't help but feel impatient.

"Here," Tony said as he handed Casper a large guitar case through the window. "You'll find everything you need in there."

"Thanks, Tony," Casper replied, flashing him a tight-lipped smile as he took the case. As Anna's fingers brushed against the cold metal latches, she knew the weight of what lay within wasn't solely due to its physical mass—the very fate of her family rested on these tools.

"Stay safe, you two," Tony said as he closed the window, his golden tooth glinting in the midday sun. With that, they began to pull away from the drive-thru. "Though... with the friendly ghost nearby," he said, jutting a thumb at Casper, "Your luck will hold out. A lot of luck."

Casper rolled his eyes again.

"We good to go, Tony?"

"Yeah... yeah, your money is good enough."

Casper gunned the engine. Anna pulled the guitar case upright, sitting it awkwardly across the dash as she opened it and scanned the contents.

Each item looked brand new. The familiar hardware gave her a strangely nostalgic feeling.

Navigating through the narrow, pothole-ridden streets, Casper and Anna shared a tense silence. The anticipation of their mission hung heavy in the air, as thick as the clouds of exhaust left behind by the rusted cars that rumbled past them. Anna clenched her jaw, her eyes flicking back and forth between the rearview mirror and the city crumbling around her.

"Alright," Casper began, breaking the silence. "The industrial district is our rendezvous location. We can't afford any slip-ups, so let's go over the plan one more time."

Anna nodded, her knuckles white as she gripped the guitar case on her lap.

"We want a ground unit and overwatch?" Casper asked.

But Anna shook her head. "You have a rifle in your trunk."

"Yeah... so?"

"I'm thinking Bangalore."

"Bangalore?" Casper said, his eyebrows ratcheting up. "You sure? Dangerous plan. If they get close..."

"Won't let 'em," Anna said.

Casper shrugged. "So both of us bird's eye view?"

"That's right."

"Hmm... well, maybe we can find a holding spot. They're not gonna bring them to the rendezvous until they see proof of the drives."

"I know that."

Casper wiped his sweaty palms on his jeans. He squinted at his phone, navigating through a series of secured apps until he located the satellite imaging software. "Got it," he muttered, holding the screen up for Anna to see.

"Zoom in on that area," Anna instructed, pointing to a cluster of buildings on the outskirts of town. As Casper did as she asked, she bit her lip and clenched her left fist, her right hand hovering ready by her side—an instinctive reaction.

"See anything interesting?" Casper asked, scanning the images as he glanced at the road. His voice was steady and so was his hand holding the phone.

Anna leaned closer, her eyes narrowing as they darted across the screen.

"Wait, what's that?" she said suddenly, tapping on a structure that appeared in the middle of the satellite footage.

"It's a water tower." Casper zoomed in further, revealing the rusted metal structure standing tall among the surrounding buildings. "Seems like a good landmark to me."

"Definitely," Anna agreed, her gaze never wavering from the screen. In her mind, she was already calculating angles and distances, planning out the best approach for their rescue mission.

Anna's left hand clenched into a tight fist, her knuckles whitening as she stared at the satellite images on Casper's phone. The water tower was an essential point of reference, but her mind raced with the implications of what would happen if they couldn't reach her sister and family in time.

"Once we find them," Anna murmured, her voice tense with urgency, "we need to make sure the bad guys don't have a chance to harm them."

Casper nodded, his brow furrowed as he shared Anna's concern. "What do you suggest?"

"Diversion," Anna replied without hesitation. Her right hand absently traced the grip of her gun holstered at her side, the weapon a familiar comfort forged by years of training. "We need to draw their attention away from my family. Need someone to lure them out."

"Thinking they won't show?"

"If they see a familiar face they will."

The two of them glanced in the rearview mirror, and Waldo went stiff.

Anna frowned at him, her eyes fixated on his nervous features. "How about some redemption, Waldo? Think you're up for a little fun?"

He stared at her, his eyes wide over his gag.

Casper chuckled as he hit the gas pedal and sped in the direction of their rendezvous.

Anna meanwhile, took one item at a time from the guitar case, examining it, testing its weight, and smiling to herself.

She pulled out a single bullet, hefted it in her hand, and then nodded once.

"You're helping, Waldo."

It wasn't a question.

Chapter 22

The moon cast a pale glow over the abandoned industrial district, barely illuminating the rusted metal of the water tower. Anna approached, clad in dark clothing that blended seamlessly with the night. She adjusted the strap of her new .50 cal sniper rifle, feeling its weight against her shoulder as she moved silently toward the rendezvous point.

"Anna, you're late," Casper whispered through the radio piece nestled in her left ear. He was always punctual, something he'd learned from their years working together in the military.

"That gate was locked," she replied, scanning the area for signs of Waldo and Casper. "Should've dropped me off at the river like I said."

"Right, and have the current sweep you away?"

She snorted. "Did you really just say that to me?"

Casper cleared his throat. "That river is stronger than it looks. Whatever. I see you now."

She turned to look for Casper on the large, concrete building across the river, where he'd set up. But she couldn't spot him. Casper, like his name suggested, knew how to become a ghost. Her eyes, trained and honed by years of observing hostile territories, caught sight of Waldo, though, crouching behind a concrete wall across the River. At least, she assumed it was Waldo, given his thin frame and recalcitrant posture. At this distance, in the dead of night, it was hard to be sure.

The river cut between the industrial zone, and she supposed it had once been used for hydropower of some sort. A large, crumbling dam held back the majority of the flowing water, but she spotted more than one crack in the structure, suggesting that safety or regulatory teams had been negligent.

"Both in position?" she asked, her voice low but steady.

"Affirmative," Casper responded. "Waldo's on ground level, and I'm up high. We've got a clear view."

"He still going through with it?"

"Hell if I know. You sure know how to pick 'em."

"I didn't. I found him wandering around my sister's burnt-out home."

"Yeah? Well, he's an asshole."

"We agree on something."

Anna's eyes scanned the ground as she moved toward the water tower, her intuition nagging at her. Something was off.

"Damn," she muttered under her breath when she noticed a crumpled potato chip wrapper skittering across the gravel. She knelt down and picked it up, the greasy residue on her fingertips irking her. Her gaze shifted to a few discarded cigarette butts nearby, their orange filters standing out starkly against the darkness.

"Guys, we may have company," she whispered into her radio, her eyes narrowing suspiciously. "I've found signs of recent activity near the tower."

"Shit," Casper replied, tension evident in his voice. "What do you want us to do?"

"Stay sharp. Keep an eye out for anything unusual." She continued forward with heightened caution, her senses on high alert.

"Copy that," Casper replied, his usually stoic tone betraying his nerves.

Anna froze mid-step when she heard faint voices coming from the direction of the water tower. She strained her ears, trying to discern their words, but they were too distant and muffled.

"Guys, I'm hearing voices near the tower," she breathed into her radio, keeping her voice low. "I can't tell who they are or where they're coming from but stay on guard."

Anna's mind raced as she weighed her options. They couldn't afford any distractions or complications tonight. She moved towards the base of the water tower, extending a hand to snatch at the nearest rung.

Gripping the cold, rusty rungs of the ladder, Anna began her ascent, each step sending small flakes of rust trickling down like a metallic rainfall. Her breaths came out in visible puffs as she climbed higher into the frigid night air. The voices grew clearer with each upward movement, confirming that two men were indeed positioned atop the water tower.

"Going up," Anna whispered into her radio, her voice steady despite the adrenaline coursing through her veins.

"Be careful," Casper cautioned.

As she neared the top, the voices became more distinct. She could make out snippets of conversation—one deep and gravelly, the other slightly higher-pitched. Listening closely, she determined they were discussing wind speed and trajectory calculations—the unmistakable chatter of a sniper and his spotter.

"Damn," Anna thought to herself, "of all the places they could've chosen..."

"Target at 2 o'clock," the spotter hissed suddenly, his voice laced with excitement. "Behind the concrete wall."

Anna's heart skipped a beat. That was Waldo's position. She had to act fast, or else he'd be taken out before they even had a chance to locate Beth and her family.

Crouching low to minimize the sound of her movements, Anna crept closer to the pair. The sniper was focused on adjusting the scope of his rifle, leaving the spotter primarily responsible for keeping an eye on their surroundings. It was a small window of opportunity, but one that Anna was determined to exploit.

"Wind's picking up," the sniper grunted, his voice barely audible over the howling gusts.

"Adjust for it," the spotter snapped, his attention still fixed on Waldo's hiding spot. "Boss said they'd come early. Worth more than our hide if you miss."

Anna silently closed the remaining distance between them, her grip tightening on the handle of her knife. She knew what had to be done.

The sniper tensed. She could see him beginning to aim. Could hear the spotter whispering final instructions.

The sniper's finger pressed on the trigger.

Anna lunged forward, her left hand gripping the handle of her knife tightly. The spotter's eyes widened, but there was no time to register the shock on his face as she drove the blade into his neck.

He choked, blood spattering across the water tower's rusty floor.

"Hey, what's—" the sniper began, but Anna cut him off by tackling him to the ground.

She hissed through clenched teeth as they grappled for control of the knife. The metal clanged against the surface beneath them, echoing into the night.

"Anna, status?" Casper's voice crackled through the radio.

She focused on the man beneath her. He was strong but slow.

"Get...off..." the sniper wheezed, his fingers digging into Anna's wrist, trying to pry the knife from her grasp.

"Anna, you okay?" Casper chimed in.

Anna struggled to keep the sniper pinned down while angling the blade for a decisive strike. His eyes widened in fear as he realized what she intended.

He tilted his head back and opened his mouth to scream, and she clapped a hand over his lips. He tried to bite her fingers, bucking his hips simultaneously.

The two of them rolled, and nearly fell under the gap in the rail encircling the top of the water tower.

Anna could feel the wind whipping against her face as they teetered dangerously close to the edge. She fought against the sniper's strength, desperately trying to maintain her hold on him and prevent him from making sound, while also keeping herself from plummeting to her death below.

"Anna! Answer me!" Casper's voice sounded urgent over the radio.

Anna gasped out, her voice strained with exertion. With a surge of adrenaline, she mustered all her remaining energy and delivered a swift kick to the sniper's crotch, sending him rolling backward.

As he struggled to regain composure, Anna seized the opportunity to scramble to her feet. The rusted encircling platform of the water tower swayed beneath her, adding an extra layer of instability to her already precarious position. She took a moment to steady herself before lunging at the sniper again, this time with an unyielding determination.

He was trying to shout again, and again, but she caught him before he could cry out.

Their bodies slammed together with a bone-crunching impact. Anna's knife slipped from her hand during the struggle, skittering across the platform and clattering over the edge. She cursed under her breath.

The sniper fought back ferociously, desperate to gain control and eliminate the threat before him. Their limbs tangled in a flurry of punches and kicks as they grappled for dominance. Blood smeared across Anna's face as she deflected blow after blow, using every ounce of strength she possessed.

She could hear Casper's frantic voice crackling through the radio, begging for an update on her status. But there was no time to respond.

She stumbled back and heard a pipe clatter at her foot.

He tried to swing the butt of his recovered rifle at her head. She ducked, and in the same motion ripped up the rusted pipe.

It was jagged on one end, weathered and worn from corrosive rainfall due to whatever the industrial zone had spat into the atmosphere once upon a time.

And with that, she plunged the serrated edge into his side. He grunted in pain.

She drove the pipe deeper.

He gasped, and then the sniper's eyes rolled back as he lost consciousness, finally releasing his grip on her.

"Two down," Anna panted, her heart still pounding. "I'm good, Casper," Anna muttered under her breath as she twisted the makeshift weapon, removing it from the sniper's side. Breathing heavily, she released her grasp, allowing his body to slump onto the cold metal surface of the water tower.

Sweat trickled down her brow as she wiped her bloodied weapon clean on the enemy sniper's clothes. She quickly stashed the pipe against the top of the ladder, wedging it over the manhole opening before turning her attention to the mission at hand.

"Two hostiles down. Let's get this show on the road," she whispered into her comms, her words punctuated with ragged breaths. The air around her was heavy with tension, but she had no time to lose.

"Copy that," Casper's voice crackled in her ear. "Setting up overwatch."

"Roger that," replied Anna, her fingers working deftly to sling the rifle sheath from over her shoulder. Then, she hastened to assemble her .50 cal sniper. The weight of the weapon felt reassuring in her hands, a familiar presence in an otherwise chaotic situation.

"Night vision attached," she murmured to herself, securing the device to her scope. Anticipation coursed through her veins as she scanned the dark landscape below, searching for any sign of movement.

Anna took a deep breath, steadying her nerves as she adjusted the tripod beneath her rifle. Her left hand gripped the barrel tightly.

"Come on, you bastards," she thought, her eyes never leaving the darkness beyond her scope. "Show yourselves."

In that moment, Anna felt a strange calm wash over her—the eye of the storm, perhaps. She knew that soon the night would erupt into chaos, but for now, she would hold her ground and wait.

The sweat on Anna's brow glistened under the crescent moon as she tightened the final screw on her night-vision attachment.

Her heart pounded in her chest, a steady rhythm that mirrored her resolve. With her left hand, she reached for her close circuit radio, the thick callouses on her fingers a testament to her many battles.

"Casper, you in position?" Anna whispered, her voice crackling through the line.

"Affirmative," Casper replied, his voice calm and collected. "Overwatch is set. I've got eyes on the entire east side of the River."

Anna allowed herself a small smile before switching channels, her finger hovering over the button. "Waldo, come in," she called, expecting an immediate response.

Silence greeted her.

Her grip on the radio tightened, knuckles turning white. "Waldo, do you copy? I need a status update."

Still, no answer.

"Dammit, Waldo," she muttered under her breath, frustration boiling beneath the surface. She couldn't afford any missteps tonight, especially from her own team. Albeit, a reluctant team in the case of Waldo Strange the Third. Taking a deep breath, she tried to shove aside her mounting worry. Worry wouldn't help Beth. Worry would only get people killed.

"Enough's enough," Anna growled, her patience wearing thin. She pressed the radio button with renewed force, her voice firm and commanding. "Waldo, respond now!"

A crackle of static filled her ear before Waldo's hesitant voice finally came through. "Uh, yeah... I'm here, Anna."

"About damn time," she thought, allowing herself a brief moment of relief before jumping back into action mode. "What took you so long? Are you in position?"

"Er, yes. I was... just double-checking my, er... the satchel you gave me," Waldo admitted sheepishly, his voice wavering slightly.

"Those aren't the real USB sticks," she snapped. "Don't think of scarpering with 'em."

"I wasn't. I wasn't, I swear!"

"Remember what I said I'd do to you if you ruined this?"

A swallow. "Yeah." His voice sounded hoarse.

"Well... I meant it. I keep my word, Waldo."

"Right."

Anna's eyes narrowed, scrutinizing the dark shadows of the industrial district. She knew that Waldo was the least experienced member of their improvised team, but she couldn't afford any slip-ups tonight. This mission was too important.

"Listen up, Waldo," she said, her voice sharp and focused. "No more delays, no more excuses. You dragged my sister's family into this mess."

"Accidentally."

"Which is why you're not in a body bag."

"Understood," he replied, sighing. "But I don't see how having me walk out like a chicken with its head cut off is going to help matters."

"Just stick to the script," she said. "Leave the rest to us."

Her mind raced with the countless ways this operation could go wrong. She forced herself to push those thoughts aside.

The night was thick with tension, the air heavy and oppressive. Anna's heart pounded in her chest, a relentless drumbeat that seemed to echo throughout the desolate industrial district. She watched as her own breath fogged up the night-vision scope of her .50 cal sniper rifle, momentarily obscuring her view. She wiped it clear with practiced efficiency; her left hand steady on the weapon despite the adrenaline coursing through her veins.

"Anna," Casper's voice crackled in her earpiece, snapping her attention back to the present. "We've got movement. A group of cars just pulled into the area. Looks like they're headed our way."

"Roger that," she whispered, her eyes scanning the darkness for any sign of the approaching vehicles. She knew they were out there, lurking in the shadows like hungry predators, but she couldn't see them yet. Not with her naked eye.

"Stay sharp, guys," she instructed, her voice firm and authoritative. "Waldo, stay behind that wall, and Casper, keep an eye on those cars. Let me know if anything changes."

As Anna peered through the night-vision scope once more, she finally spotted the headlights of the approaching convoy, their ghostly green glow cutting through the darkness like ethereal knives. Her breath caught in her throat as she realized just how close they were—closer than she'd anticipated.

"Damn it," she muttered under her breath, struggling to keep her mounting fear at bay. This was it. The moment they'd been preparing for. There was no turning back now.

"Anna," Casper's voice crackled again, the urgency in his tone sending a shiver down her spine. "They're almost here. I wasn't expecting this many."

She counted the vehicles; her eyes narrowed.

There were six of them, their black exteriors gleaming with a sinister aura under the pale moonlight. Anna's grip tightened on her sniper rifle, her finger hovering over the trigger. The weight of responsibility settled heavy on her shoulders as she realized the lives of her sister's family and the success of the mission depended on her next move.

"Waldo, don't let them see you," Anna whispered urgently into the radio. "Stay hidden until I give the signal. Casper, be ready to provide cover fire if needed."

She took a deep breath, steadying herself as she surveyed the approaching convoy. These were no ordinary vehicles. They were military-style jeeps, complete with bulletproof glass and reinforced metal doors. They were likely decommissioned, as she didn't recognize them. But someone had put the vehicles to use.

The convoy of cars drew nearer, their headlights casting eerie shadows across the abandoned buildings and rusted machinery that littered the industrial district. As Anna watched them approach, she couldn't help but feel a sense of foreboding wash over her.

"Here they come," she murmured, her voice barely audible even to herself. "God help us all."

"Anna... Anna, Waldo's off comms."

"No, I'm not, asshole," Waldo retorted suddenly, his voice staticky. "I dropped the earpiece."

"Focus, both of you," she snapped. "Waldo, you got the drives?"

"Yeah," he said, sullen. "What if... what if they shoot me?"

"What if I do?" she returned.

"What if—" he began, but she didn't hear the rest of it. Her phone suddenly began to ring.

She tensed, staring down at where the device rested on the frame of the metal tower. She let out a faint breath of air. The device continued to glow.

"John" was calling her.

The kidnappers were on the line.

She tensed briefly, double-checked her scope, and then answered the phone, scowling into the dark.

Chapter 23

Anna breathed deeply, the phone pressed against her ear as she stared through the night-vision scope towards the men below. In one ear, she could hear Casper steadying his own breath.

Her mind flashed back.

Casper hadn't always been a rotund, ex-SEAL. Once upon a time, he'd been one of the best shots in the platoon. The two of them had often competed with one another in shooting competitions. The same dollar, which they'd called an "honor buck" had exchanged hands more than once.

She found the sound of his breathing oddly comforting.

For five years now, she'd lived on the move.

Had lived in a home with wheels, or campsites at national parks. She dealt in cash and lived off-grid as much as possible. She didn't trust phones and only picked up burners when she needed them for a job.

Like this one.

She didn't trust the device and held it in a tight grip.

Her eyes scanned the procession of six armored vehicles in the distance.

She tensed, waiting, the phone pressed to her ear.

"Anna Gabriel?" said the voice on the other line.

It was not the deep voice of John, nor the snively, banker's voice of the other John.

This was a soft, almost falsetto voice. It enunciated the words clearly and had a sort of singsong quality that almost made her think of a British accent, though he sounded American. It was a strange voice, a cultured one.

And she instantly knew she didn't like it.

"Who's this?"

"I don't give my name," said the voice softly.

"I don't talk to strangers," she returned.

"Ah, but am I a stranger? I have someone here who knows you well. Say hello, Beth."

Anna tensed, and then her sister's voice came through, desperate and frightened. "Anna—Anna, please! They have the kids. Oh, God. I'm so sorry, Anna. They have Sarah and Tony. They have Tom!" Her voice was rising in panic as she spoke, desperate and pained.

Anna felt each word drive a shard of ice through her chest. She swallowed briefly, trying to steady her nerves.

"It's going to be okay, Beth," Anna said softly.

Then, the cultured voice returned. He sounded almost amused, and a little bit tired. "This has gone on long enough, Ms. Gabriel. You know what I want, and I know that you have it. Why tarry any longer? Where is my money?"

"It's on two separate flash drives," she said simply. "I'll give you one. You give me my sister. And once we're safe, I'll give you the other."

"No. No, that's not how this is going to work, Ms. Gabriel. You give me everything I ask for, and then you can have your sister and her family. We do things my way."

"The thing is," Anna said, "I don't trust you." She remembered what she'd been told about the albino. A man like a shark. That's what Waldo had said.

Then again, Waldo had said a lot of things, and the grifter was often scared of his own shadow.

"Do we have an accord?" said the voice.

Anna didn't reply at first. Quietly, in her other ear, Casper was giving her a rundown of what he could see from his angle.

"I think I see the speaker, Anna," he was saying. "Middle vehicle. There's a woman in the front seat with him. He's got a knife pressed to her neck."

Anna listened to this and tensed with each subsequent word, but she gave no indication to the phone that she'd been told any of this.

Instead, she simply said, "Alright. I guess you leave me with no choice."

She had to get Beth alone. And the bulletproof glass on the vehicles changed things. If the man remained in the car with her sister, there'd be no clean shot. She needed the Albino out of the vehicle.

"Fine," she replied, her voice steady. "I'll give you what you want. But first, I need proof that they're still alive."

There was a moment of silence before the Albino responded. "You just spoke to your sister."

"The others," Anna said. "Her children. Her husband."

"Ah, well... I'm afraid they're not here."

"That wasn't the deal," Anna said suddenly.

"I'm afraid I don't trust you, Ms. Gabriel. For one, I don't see you. Where are you?"

She remained steady, still staring towards the ground.

"I've done my research into you, Ms. Gabriel," he said softly, the words delicate and soft as if he were peeling back the lairs of some ripe piece of fruit. "I know you like taking your enemies at a distance, hmm? You're not on that old chemical plant roof, are you? It seems like a good spot for a sniper."

She stared across the river towards the large, gray building.

Casper was on that roof.

She didn't say anything, still watching through her scope.

The procession of vehicles had now come to a complete stop.

Men were now emerging from the vehicles, weapons held tightly, eyes attentive and alert as they glanced about.

"A Navy SEAL," said the man quietly. "Your sister tells me that if I don't let her children go, you'll kill me."

"I'll do worse than that," Anna said matter-of-factly.

"Is there anything worse than death? I wonder," the albino murmured. "I truly wonder..." He trailed off. "Now, you've heard your sister. She's alive. Let's trade. I'll give your sister to you now, as a show of good faith, and once her husband unlocks the files, I'll release the rest of them."

"That wasn't the deal."

"Well it's the deal now, isn't it?" The voice tensed. "Now stop wasting my time, or I'll start returning your sister to you a piece at a time."

Anna shivered at the way the voice had gone suddenly cold. She shifted her position on the water tower, and now, braced against the railing, she had a clear view of where the man was with Beth.

She glanced over at the roof of the building across the river. Her phone was on speaker, so Casper would've heard the guess that he was situated in that particular building, and judging by his lack of comments, she scanned the stairwell at the base of the run-down structure.

Then she spotted him. Casper was moving hurriedly, already hastening across the street.

The out-of-shape SEAL still booked it, rushing towards the building opposite them; he darted into the bottom floor, and she was able to track his movements as he exited into a back alley and continued on his way.

Quickly, she put her speaker on mute, and said into her radio, "You moving?"

"Double-time."

"Good. I think I see two of those gunmen moving towards your last post."

"Already saw 'em. Do I engage?"

"No. Not yet," Anna said quickly. "We need to get Beth alone. We need to find a way to lure him out."

"Give him what he wants. Doubt he'll trust a lackey with those flash drives. Not after all this."

"Okay. Okay, stand by."

She unmuted herself on the phone, and said, "Waldo is coming to you."

"Waldo?" A snort. "That fool? I should've known he'd double-crossed me."

"He has the flash drives."

"Where?"

"He's coming, but he'll only give them to you personally."

Anna waited, tense.

If the albino was the man in the car with Beth, then he'd have to leave her in order to fetch the USB drives. This was a game of slim margins, and she knew it. Time was of the essence, and it was rapidly diminishing.

"Step out into the open so you can shoot me? I don't think so," sneered the man.

"You want your money or not?" Anna demanded.

"I will kill your sister."

"No, you won't," Anna retorted with more confidence than she felt. "Eight million dollars, sir. You're willing to throw that away because you're scared of little old me? Not very impressive of you, is it?"

She intentionally was goading him, and she allowed a sneer into her voice, hoping he felt every ounce of the oozing contempt.

The man swallowed briefly, and she could feel him weighing his options.

"The moment you emerge, you get your money. That's that."

"Any tricks and they all die," he said.

And suddenly, he hung up.

She tensed, watching through her scope, willing the man in the car to emerge.

She watched as he gestured at other figures from the other vehicles. Six gunmen hastened over.

Briefly, she allowed herself to wonder where this firepower was coming from. Who was this man?

But then, she watched in excitement as the door to the car holding her sister swung open. Beth remained in the back seat, and then the door was slammed shut. Two guards of the six were positioned by the door, guarding Beth.

She finally had a good look at the albino; though through a night-vision lens, it wasn't a clean look.

His hair was as white as his skin, and his pale eyes almost seemed to glow in the darkness. His features were sharp and angular, giving him an otherworldly appearance.

Anna watched as the albino spoke to Beth through the car window. Beth's eyes were filled with fear, but Anna knew Beth would do whatever it took to protect their family.

As Anna continued to observe, she noticed a slight movement near the final building across the river. She tensed. Two gunmen had emerged from the nearest Jeep, and one had paused to take a leak. Another figure was sneaking behind the second gunman, moving in a low crouch, sticking to the shadows. It was Casper, slowly making his way towards the guards. He was hidden in the dark, using every bit of stealth his now rotund form would allow.

Anna's heart pounded in her chest as she watched Casper silently take down one of the guards with a swift strike to the throat. The other guard seemed unaware of what was happening until it was too late. He continued whizzing against the wall, but then the ex-SEAL's arm snaked around his throat, and Casper swiftly incapacitated him, rendering both guards unconscious.

Anna took a deep breath.

Casper spoke in the radio, her ear itching as the receiver buzzed.

"Moving in closer. Outlook compromised."

"Roger," she replied, as the albino had already hung up. She quickly adjusted her scope and aimed at the albino as he gestured for the four other gunmen who'd approached to surround him as a sort of walking human shield.

Then, he began moving toward a small, cement bridge that arched over the river.

She switched radio channels. "Waldo... now's your turn."

She returned her attention towards where the con artist was still creeping behind the same concrete wall as before. He looked downright terrified and was shaking like a leaf. All his talk of being *ataraxic*, of being *fearless*, Anna couldn't believe she'd ever even considered that lie.

Nothing he said was true.

And she was beginning to rue bringing him along.

Would he turn on them? It seemed likely.

"Waldo. Now," she said. Then, exhaling slowly, she said, "My sister is there. Her kids are going to die. Waldo, I swear, I've got you covered. If any of them try to shoot you, I'll protect you. I promise. Please," she added.

The man exhaled deeply, then pushed slowly to his feet, nodding as he did.

He tapped a finger at his ear, burying the radio receiver even deeper.

"Stop doing that," she whispered quickly.

He lowered his hand. Then, trembling, he moved towards the group by the vehicles. He picked up his pace, approaching the bridge.

The solitary, gangly figure of the conman drew near where the albino was flanked by four gunmen.

Anna kept glancing towards the men by her sister's car. They remained outside the vehicle.

Excitement flared.

"Alright, Waldo," she said softly, "When I say, you're going to jump."

"Wh-what?"

"When I tell you, jump in the river. Clear?"

"The river? You didn't say anything about a river," he said, half turning as if he wanted to run away.

"Don't turn now or they'll shoot you," she said. "Trust me. I'll protect you if you stick to the plan. The river has a strong current. It'll drop you off on the bank back where we parked the car. Trust me."

"Trustworthy people don't usually have to keep repeating the sentiment," he retorted.

"Stop talking to me. Give him the flash drives."

"He'll know they're fake," Waldo whispered.

"Just do it. You'll be fine."

"I'm approaching the vehicle," Casper said, coming through on the other channel.

"Copy that," she returned. "Wait until my signal."

"I'm going for the car," Casper said. "Two down behind me, and two searching the roof of the chemical plant. That's my four anyhow."

"Yeah. Good call," she said quickly. "But just wait. Wait until my signal."

She kept track of everything, feeling her body tense until her stomach ached. Her sister, alone in the jeep, but guarded by two gunmen just outside the vehicle. Casper, sneaking across a spot in the dam that overlapped the water with a shelf of concrete.

And Waldo, trembling as he slowly approached the small bridge and the five killers.

All of it was moving so swiftly that Anna felt as if at any moment she might lose the thread. The albino would know the USB drives were fakes. But how long until he realized it?

She'd given Waldo her word. She'd have to keep him safe.

But if push came to shove, she'd throw everything in the fire to protect Beth.

Casper was halfway across the concrete shelf. He'd almost reached the car.

He waited in the shadows of an outcrop, peering towards the two gunmen, his sidearm clutched tightly.

Everything was on a tightrope.

Anna's heart raced as she watched the events unfold before her. The tension in the air was palpable, and every fiber of her being urged her to act. But she knew that timing was crucial, and she had to wait for the perfect moment to make her move.

The albino and his men walked towards the small cement bridge, unaware of the danger that lurked nearby. Anna adjusted her scope, focusing on the albino's every move. She knew she had to take him out if they were to have any chance of succeeding.

"Waldo," she whispered urgently into her radio. "Now!"

With bated breath, she watched as Waldo hesitated for a moment, fear evident in his eyes. He then flung the fake flash drives onto the bridge.

This briefly distracted the albino, as he lunged for them. Then, a flicker of determination ignited within Waldo's trembling form. He took a deep breath and leapt off the bridge into the river below.

The albino tensed, stunned, one hand closed around the USB drives that had landed on the cement.

As Waldo disappeared beneath the surface, Anna's heart skipped a beat. She knew she had to trust in their plan, that Waldo would resurface downstream and make it back to safety. Now it was up to Casper to create a diversion while they rescued Beth.

With lightning speed, Casper made his move. He swiftly incapacitated one of the guards standing by Beth's car with a well-aimed blow to the back of the neck. His sidearm leapt up, shooting the second man through the head.

Anna was already opening fire.

Her first bullet was aimed toward the albino's heart, but he ducked behind the cement wall and dragged one of his guards in front of him.

This unfortunate gunman caught a bullet in the gut, and he fell over, a fifty caliber hole in his gut.

Anna was already moving, another round chambered.

Three more gunmen remained on the bridge. They were diving for cover as well. The albino squeezed off a shot, but he was aiming blindly.

She spotted the two men assigned to the roof across the river.

She swiveled, aiming towards them before they could call out her location.

With precise accuracy, Anna took down the two gunmen on the roof, their bodies crumpling to the ground. The sound of gunfire echoed through the air, creating chaos and confusion among the remaining attackers.

The albino, realizing his plan was unraveling, made a desperate attempt to escape. He shoved an injured guard aside and sprinted towards a nearby Jeep parked just beyond the bridge. Bullets whizzed past him as Anna continued to fire, determined to bring him down.

Casper emerged from the shadows, joining Anna in the crossfire. Together, they unleashed a barrage of bullets towards the remaining gunmen on the bridge. One by one, they fell to the ground, their bodies limp and lifeless.

More gunmen were emerging from the vehicles in the back of the procession.

And then Anna heard a horrifying sound.

The thumping of helicopter blades against the sky.

She turned, staring in horror as a helicopter sped towards them, moving over the industrial district. The albino had expected her to take a lookout post. He'd come prepared.

The helicopter was a civilian one, with no mounted gun, but the rattle of weapons fire suggested there were armed assailants in the heli as well.

She cursed. She had to move. The water tower was compromised, which meant she'd lose sight of her sister for now. In her final glance, she saw Casper was already crawling into the driver's seat. Beth stayed put, staring at it all in horror.

The gunmen from the back of the procession had spotted Casper, now, and were aiming toward the bulletproof Jeep. Five men opened fire, and bullets slammed into the armored vehicle, causing it to shake.

Anna was able to squeeze off two more shots, taking down two more of the attackers, but then the gunmen in the heli spotted her from the muzzle flash. Bullets slammed into the water tower, and one hit the barrel of her newly acquired Baretta.

Anna felt a searing pain in her hand as the weapon was torn from her hand and sent clattering over the railing. But she clenched her teeth and refused to let it slow her down as she pulled her sidearm. She returned fire, aiming for the gunmen in the chopper, determined to take them down before they could do any more damage.

She spotted Casper as he gunned the engine of the bulletproof Jeep, swerving to avoid the hail of bullets that continued to rain down upon them. Beth clutched onto the door handle, her frame so small and vulnerable from this distance.

Where were her children? Where was Tom? A small part of Anna hoped this all hadn't been a terrible mistake.

Anna flung herself at the ladder, sliding down the metal frame. Bullets skimmed off the water tower, hitting rungs, and tearing through metal. She hit the ground, squeezing off two more shots.

A man fell from the chopper, tumbling like a ragdoll caught in a gust of wind. As another bullet hit the windshield, the helicopter swayed dangerously, its pilot struggling to maintain control. Anna saw her opportunity and sprinted towards the Jeep, her heart revolting in her chest.

Casper had managed to navigate the chaotic onslaught of bullets and was now close to the bridge. He swung open the back door of the Jeep, urging Anna to get inside. "Come on!" he shouted. "Come on!"

Anna leaped into the passenger seat just as Casper slammed his foot on the gas pedal, propelling them forward with a screech of tires. The Jeep barreled across the bridge, bullets ricocheting off its armored exterior.

As they crossed the bridge, Anna glanced back at the chaos unfolding behind them. The albino's men were scrambling to regroup, their leader left abandoned with no means of escape as the damaged helicopter hovered above him.

Anna's hand throbbed from where her rifle had been ripped from her palm, blood seeping through her fingers. She pressed her hand against her leg, willing herself to push through the pain. There was no time for weakness now—they weren't out of danger yet.

Anna turned towards her sister.

Beth was staring at her in shock, her face streaked with ash and soot. Her eyes were wide, pleading. "We have to go back!" Beth screamed. "The kids. Tom!"

Anna shook her head. "Do you have any clue where they are?"

"Yes!" Beth yelled. "He threatened..." She was hyperventilating now, her breaths coming fast and uneven. "He threatened..." She swallowed. "To throw them out of... of..." she looked ready to pass out. All the adrenaline-fueled mama bear courage that had brought her to this point seemed to be slowly seeping away now that she had backup.

But Beth pointed towards the helicopter, her finger trembling.

Anna looked up, staring in horror.

"They're on that?"

"Yes!" Beth screamed.

Anna cursed, glancing at Casper. Casper just shook his head, turning the steering wheel sharply and swerving over the bridge.

The albino was nowhere to be seen.

More gunmen were surging towards them. More bullets whizzed off the hood of their car.

Beth's eyes rolled back, and she let out a shaky breath. "I knew you'd come," she whispered. She stared weakly at her sister. Anna was still turned, meeting her younger sister's gaze. How long had it been since they'd seen each other face to face?

So many years...

Anna felt a jolt of regret.

"I knew you'd come," Beth repeated.

"We're going to get you safe," Anna said. "It's going to be okay. I promise."

Beth's eyes fluttered shut, and her head lolled to the side.

"Beth!" Anna said sharply. "Beth!"

But her sister was unconscious. Anna reached out, checking desperately for her sister's pulse. "Was she shot?" she demanded of Casper.

"No. Fatigue or she's drugged. Or shock. Or all three," he rattled off. He cursed again as he spun the vehicle, avoiding a gunman who'd emerged from the building where Anna had spotted Casper knock two of the albino's men unconscious.

Suddenly, Anna froze.

As she'd turned, she spotted a figure.

The albino was standing on the bridge now, the horizon behind him engulfed in flames rising up from exploded Jeeps. Ash from the fires lingered in the air. The rushing of the river competed with the churning helicopter blades, seeking some sort of dominance.

The helicopter was descending slowly now, moving towards the albino. Tom and the kids were on board that thing. How the hell were they supposed to reach the heli?

The albino was staring toward the fleeing vehicle, and Anna thought, briefly, that he met her gaze. He was holding the USB sticks in one hand. She could see them glinting where they dangled like dog tags.

He spat, tossing the flash drives over the rail into the river. His face was creased in streaks of blood from his injured and dead men. But in one hand, he held a rifle. It looked far too big for him. He held it awkwardly as he lifted it.

Anna stared over the back seat.

Time seemed to slow, even as Casper maneuvered fiercely.

The albino raised his gun.

She tensed.

"No," she whispered. She realized what he was about to do. "No!" she screamed.

He fired.

He wasn't aiming at them, though.

Instead, he'd taken aim at the fuel tank of the limping heli.

She stared in absolute horror as his bullets struck the tank.

The fuel tank erupted into a ball of flames, engulfing the helicopter in an inferno. The explosion was deafening, echoing through the bridge as the helicopter plummeted towards the river below. Anna's heart sank as she watched the burning wreckage crash into the water, consumed by the river's current.

"No!" Anna screamed, her voice drowned out by the chaos. She struggled against Casper's firm grip on the steering wheel, in a moment of madness wanting desperately to dive into the water and search for any sign of her family members. But Casper held her back, his eyes filled with concern.

"We can't go back now," he said sternly, his voice barely audible over the roaring flames. "We have to keep moving."

"They might be alive! They might be—"

"You want your sister dead too?" he snapped. "Stop. Now!"

Anna collapsed back into her seat, tears streaming down her face. The pain in her hand seemed insignificant compared to the ache in her chest. She clenched her fist, feeling a mixture of anger and despair coursing through her veins.

She glanced back.

Beth remained motionless in the backseat. Mercifully, she hadn't witnessed the explosion.

"Maybe they weren't on board," Casper said quickly. "Maybe they weren't."

"Then why would he shoot it?" Anna demanded.

"Anger? Petty violence? He told her they were. Maybe he wants her to think they're dead!"

As they sped away from the scene, Anna felt weak all of a sudden. Exhausted. "What if they're dead?" she whispered.

Casper glanced at her, then back at the road. "Then you're sister is going to need you to be stronger than ever. Sit back. We're almost out."

He veered sharply, avoiding a bump in the road.

She spotted a water-slicked figure up ahead, teeth chattering, stumbling towards them. Waldo Strange had survived the fall.

For a moment, she wanted to lash out at him. He'd put Beth's name in the crossfire of the albino. He'd caused this...

But the hatred felt empty.

She knew it wasn't really true. Waldo had underestimated the albino. The same as Anna. She hadn't been prepared. She'd failed the mission.

What if Tom was still alive? What if the kids hadn't been on that chopper?

It was slim hope.

Very slim.

Waldo stumbled towards the car, and Casper flung open the back door, leaning over his seat.

"Get in!" Casper commanded.

Trembling, teeth chattering, Waldo slipped into the car.

"I did it!" he exclaimed. "Did you see me?" He crowed. "I flung that USB drive and dove like a champion. That was epic!"

He was grinning now, basking in the glow of an after-combat high.

Anna didn't have the heart to speak to him. He'd gone into the lion's den with those flash drives. Beth might've been dead if not for him.

She sunk in her seat, unsure where to direct her anger, her terror, her pain. So instead, Anna simply closed her eyes, releasing a long pent-up breath.

Chapter 24

Beth lay in the bed of the C-class RV, eyes still closed, but her head now bandaged.

Anna winced as Casper wrapped her wounded hand. "Hold still," Casper said firmly.

Morning light was now trickling through the blinds. Waldo Strange had been dropped off at his motel, and he'd disappeared.

Hours later, they were now in the mountains, away from the news crews and police sirens raiding the small war zone. The radio was nothing but news bulletins about the shootout. Anna had turned the radio off hours ago.

Beth was still sleeping, and Anna dreaded the moment her sister would wake. The moment Anna would have to tell her the news.

Anna tried to push away the overwhelming guilt that consumed her. She should have been more prepared, more cautious. She should have anticipated the albino's viciousness, his willingness to destroy everything in his path. If only she had acted sooner if only she had been able to protect her family.

"Stop that," Casper muttered. He finished bandaging her hand and leaned back, frowning at her.

Both of them were still soot-stained and smelling of gunpowder. Both of them looked exhausted.

Anna glanced in the rearview mirror, getting a good look at her blood and ash-streaked features. Tears had carved a path through the mess. She looked away, biting her lower lip if only to allow the pain to center her.

"It wasn't your fault," Casper said softly.

"Bullshit," she murmured.

"I mean it. They really might be alive," Casper said. "Maybe he was playing you. You told me there were gunmen in that chopper, right? It was a small bird. There aren't that many seats. I doubt three more passengers were on it."

"Beth said they were."

"Because the asshole told her that."

"Why did he shoot it then?" Anna demanded, turning to look at Casper. "Why shoot it if it only held his own men?"

Casper trailed off. "I told you... maybe he was pissed they let you get away. Maybe he was trying to sell a bluff."

"You don't believe that."

"We don't know, is my point," Casper said firmly.

He leaned back in the passenger seat.

Anna sat on the driver's side, but the RV was idling. Beth was visible in the bedroom in the back, and every so often Anna would look over to make sure her sister was still safe.

"So?" Casper said softly.

"So what?"

"The job's done," Casper said meaningfully. When Anna didn't reply, he tilted his head and added, "Why did you get discharged?"

Anna scoffed. "You want that now?"

"Deal's a deal. Besides, sulking isn't going to help anything."

"I'm not sulking."

"Then pay up, Guardian."

Anna sighed. She knew he was trying to distract her. But maybe that's just what she needed. She peered through the windshield, scanning the forest at the foot of the mountain where they'd parked. Yosemite was only a few minutes north.

The Sierras were gorgeous. Each peak seemed to touch the sky, a majestic display of nature's power. Anna had always found solace in the mountains, but now they only served as a reminder of her failure.

"I got discharged because I made a mistake," Anna admitted, her voice barely above a whisper.

"What mistake?"

"I trusted a supervisor," she said simply.

"You mean Captain—"

"Don't say his name," she cut him off. "I've spent years trying to..." Anna took a short, huffing breath, blinking as her mouth cut into a hard line. "Just don't say it."

"Right," Casper said softly. "We'll just call him the asshole, then."

"Yeah. Him."

"So you trusted him? What, romantically?"

"What?" she looked at him, momentarily forgetting her burbling guilt. "That's what you—? Gross."

Casper held up his hands apologetically. But the motion was a bit too fast, a touch too animated.

Anna sighed. "You don't need to keep doing that."

"Doing what?"

"Trying to distract me. To make me feel better."

"Ah, but it's working." He winked at her.

"You want an answer or not?" She allowed herself a small smile, rolling her neck before continuing. "Anyway... I trusted his intel. Led some good people into a trap. Two of them didn't make it out."

"So how was that your fault?"

"Wasn't. Me punching his teeth out was."

"Oh... I see."

She shrugged. "That wasn't all. I stole his Corvette."

"You what?" he stared. "You stole Capt--er, asshole's car? He loved that thing."

"Yeah, well, he shouldn't have been allowed to have it on base anyway. Bullshit special permission, getting his brother to drive it on as a contractor. Everyone knew what he was doing."

"No shit."

"So what happened with the corvette?"

Anna allowed herself a small smile. "It hit an IED."

"You're joking."

"Nah. I may have... found one first. And then rolled it into it. But, you know... same result."

Casper snorted, leaning back and staring at her with awe and admiration. "Damn. That was worth it. You really stole Captain asshole's Corvette and blew it up?"

"After punching him. Yeah. For a day they thought he'd died."

"Why'd they think that?"

"Because they found two of his teeth at the scene."

Casper stared, and then he began to laugh. "The teeth you knocked out with the punch?"

"The same," she replied, allowing herself a weary smile.

She closed her eyes again.

"So you got discharged... lucky you weren't in prison."

"Yeah, well... his revenge got me my settlement deal."

"What'd he do?"

She shook her head. "Nothing comes free, Casper. That story wasn't part of our deal."

She leaned back, eyes still closed, and exhaled slowly.

She could feel Casper watching her, and she could also feel a cool breeze coming through the open window.

"They might still be alive, Anna," Casper said.

"Maybe."

"We can find out."

"We?"

She heard him shift. "I mean... you gotta give me the rest of that story."

She opened one eye, studying Casper. "Thanks," she said.

"Aw, don't get all soft on me, Gabriel. We're gonna have to kick some ass."

Anna nodded, frowning to herself.

With or without Casper, if there was even a chance her family hadn't been on that chopper, then she was determined to find out.

She owed Beth that much. She'd rescued her sister.

But the story didn't end there.

Anna pictured the albino standing on the bridge, that gun in his hand, hatred in his eyes... She felt a shiver down her spine and doubted that was the last time their paths would cross.

Only next time, she was determined that only one of them would make it out of the encounter alive.

The End.

Book 2 is waiting for you. Scan the QR code with your phone to find your copy of Guardian's Wrath.

What's Next for Anna?

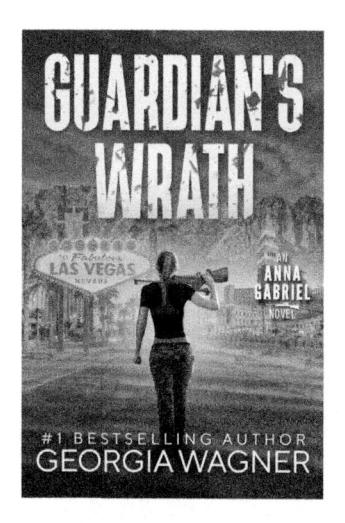

When two FBI agents are brutally murdered, all fingers point towards ex-Navy Seal, Anna Gabriel.

But Anna knows better; her old nemesis, the ruthless human trafficker Abdo Sahid, whom she once failed to bring to justice, has surfaced in the United States. This revelation propels Anna on a perilous journey to Las Vegas, a city shimmering with lights and lurking shadows, where she must confront her past failures and seize a second chance to stop Sahid once and for all. In a race against time and amidst the dazzling yet dangerous backdrop of Sin City, Anna is determined to right the wrongs of her past, but the stakes are higher than ever.

Also by Georgia Wagner

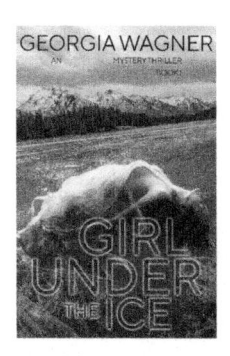

Once a rising star in the FBI, with the best case closure rate of any investigator, Ella Porter is now exiled to a small gold mining town bordering the wilderness of Alaska. The reason for her new assignment? She allowed a prolific serial killer to escape custody.

But what no one knows is that she did it on purpose.

The day she shows up in Nome, bags still unpacked, the wife of the richest gold miner in town goes missing. This is the second woman to vanish in as many days. And it's up to Ella to find out what happened.

Assigning Ella to Nome is no accident, either. Though she swore she'd never return, Ella grew up in the small, gold mining town, treated like royalty as a child due to her own family's wealth. But like all gold tycoons, the Porter family secrets are as dark as Ella's own.

Also by Georgia Wagner

The skeletons in her closet are twitching...

Genius chess master and FBI consultant Artemis Blythe swore she'd never return to the misty Cascade Mountains. Her father—a notorious serial killer, responsible for the deaths of seven women—is now imprisoned, in no small part due to a clue she provided nearly fifteen years ago.

And now her father wants his vengeance.

A new serial killer is hunting the wealthy and the elite in the town of Pinelake. Artemis' father claims he knows the identity of the killer, but he'll only tell daughter dearest. Against her will, she finds herself forced back to her old stomping grounds.

Once known as a child chess prodigy, now the locals only think of her as 'The Ghostkiller's' daughter.

In the face of a shamed family name and a brother involved with the Seattle mob, Artemis endeavours to use her tactical genius to solve the baffling case.

Hunting a murderer who strikes without a trace, if she fails, the next skeleton in her closet will be her own.

Also by Georgia Wagner

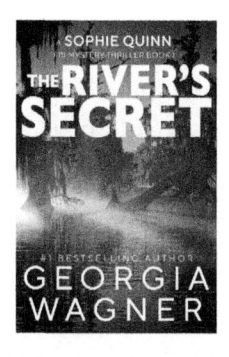

A cold knife, a brutal laugh.

Then the odds-defying escape.

Once a hypnotist with her own TV show, now, Sophie Quinn works as a full-time consultant for the FBI. Everything changed six years ago. She can still remember that horrible night. Slated to be the River Killer's tenth victim, she managed to slip her bindings and barely escape where so many others failed. Her sister wasn't so lucky.

And now the killer is back.

Two PHDs later, she's now a rising star at the FBI. Her photographic memory helps solve crimes, but also helps her to never forget. She saw the River Killer's tattoo. She knows what he sounds like. And now, ten years later, he's active again.

Sophie Quinn heads back home to the swamps of Louisiana, along the Mississippi River, intent on evening the score and finding the man who killed her sister. It's been six years since she's been home, though. Broken relationships and shattered dreams exist among the bayous, the rivers, the waterways and swamps of Louisiana; can Sophie find her way home again? Or will she be the River Killer's next victim to float downstream?

Want to know more?

Want to see what else the Greenfield authors have written? Go to the website.

Home - Greenfield Press

Or sign up to our newsletter where you will get sneak peeks, exclusive giveaways, behind the scenes content, and more. Plus, you'll be notified of Fan Pricing events when they occur and get exclusive offers from other authors.

Click the link or copy it carefully into your web browser.

Newsletter - Greenfield Press

Prefer social media? Join our thriving Facebook community.

Want to join the inner circle where you can keep up to date with everything? This is a free page on Facebook where you can hang out with likeminded individuals and enjoy discussing my books. There is cake too (but only if you bring it).

Facebook

About the Author

Georgia Wagner worked as a ghost writer for many, many years before finally taking the plunge into self-publishing. Location and character are two big factors for Georgia, and getting those right allows the story to flow seamlessly onto the page. And flow it does, because Georgia is so prolific a new term is required to describe the rate at which nerve-tingling stories find their way into print.

When not found attached to a laptop, Georgia likes spending time in local arboretums, among the trees and ponds. An avid cultivator of orchids, begonias, and all things floral, Georgia also has a strong penchant for art, paintings, and sculptures.